The Phalanx of Houston . . .

This ain't Dickens. But maybe you will like it. In this dark confessional comedy/light blowhard drama (though probably more sad than anything), our main guy and struggling lunatic Bjorn — American drifter with his G.E.D., sometimes bartender, recreational poet, terrible Buddhist — tells his short-sweet story from a quiet Colorado mountain town. Looking back to a few shit days the summer before, Bjorn unearths how his good friend, a professional soccer player who sat on the bench with glory and a crap haircut, has died. A story of why, during these few shit days, this weekend plus overtime, Bjorn, as he spouts it, had to return to his home city of Houston, Texas: to reconnect, to see if his memories match up — with his alcoholic father and everything else. Bjorn's return to associated bizarro hellishness is not Dante's Inferno, but this is Houston after all: the country's fourth-largest city that, in recent memory, has been designated the nation's most obese, most polluted, and with the worst traffic — a convoluted mess of a sometimes nightmarish concrete and sinstrewn sprawl, denigrated by the constant wet hot humid piss of a Texas beast . . . loooooong ways from perfection . . . yet, Bjorn, in his Return to Houston, has to reconcile this confusion. He has to forgive his return. Along the way he learns some things. And along the way he chooses to let it go. Breathe it out. You can go home again, and it fucking blows . . . mostly . . . but, as he comes to realize, beatitude and mercy are in the blow.

Books of Ancient Philosophy EMP Recommends to Un-Fuck Your Head

#Beer by Ezhno Martin

Test Swan by J.I.B & Gavin McGuire

Zen and the Art of Motorcycle Maintenance by Robert M. Pirsig

Trail Her Trash by Lola Nation

One Flew Over the Cuckoo's Nest by Ken Kesey

Awakening the Buddha Within by Lama Surya Das

Bury My Heart in the Gutter by Dan Denton

Modern Motorcycle Mechanics by John Bernard Nicholson

Dumpster Fire by Boyd Leonard

Those who Favor Fire, Those who Pray to Fire by Ben Brindise & Justin Karcher

Parade of Malfeasance by Joseph Goosey

My Lungs Are a Dive Bar by Walter Moore

XXX BAG OF DICKS. CORNBREAD. RIVER TWICE IS A SWAMP. HOUSTON. BROKEN BOTTLES. I NEVER WENT TO PROM. FOR HANK. HJDHJ. WAYLON KNOWS. CANCER STICKS. MALANX. BLOWHARD. MY LUNGS ARE A DANCE PARTY. XYX. MY EX-GIRLFRIEND GAVE SOME DUDE A BLOWJOB AT A GAS STATION. BJORN LEONARD. BJORN. LEONARD'S X. ALWAYS KNOW A MAN'S CREDENTIALS. VANCE WAS AN ASSHOLE. I APOLOGIZE. THE PHALANX. LOST A FRIEND, GAINED A FATHER. THREE CHEERS FOR THE GODDAMNED PHALANX. THE GENTLEMAN PHALANX. LONG SMOOTH WEEKEND. HUMID BEAST. ALUMINUM BARDO. **THE PHALANX OF HOUSTON.** STEVE MCQUEEN THIS. A GODDAMNED GENTLEMAN. SOME KIND OF FUNERAL. SO THEY DO. NO NEED FOR FORGIVENESS. GIRL NAMED MERLE. AFTER THE GREYHOUND. **A Novel.** CHICKENSHIT BINGO. PLEASE REMEMBER THE MALANX. LETTER TO A GIRL NAMED MERLE. FEW DAYS IN HOUSTON. TOOK THE BUS BACK TO HOUSTON. GREYHOUND STOPPED IN HOUSTON. THE BELL JAR WAS AN ILLUSION **WALTER MOORE.** FLYING SHOES. COULD HAVE BEEN WORSE. LONE STAR IN THE BARDO. VINTAGE. RELEASE THE PHALANX. THIS ONE'S FOR VIRGINIA. LONE STAR COWBOY. THREE DAYS IN PARADISE. FLOWERS SOAKED IN LONE STAR. K-HOLE DIARY. WOKE UP NEXT TO A DUMPSTER. RIVER TWICE IS A SWAMP. BAG O' GAG HEART **XXX.**

Columbus, Ohio
empbooks.com

Copyright © 2021 Walter Moore

We find discussions of our rights — as publishers and authors — to be laughable, all things considered. Please claim this work as your own. Please republish it and sell it on street corners. Please include our material in ALL of your get-rich-quick schemes. All we ask is that you accept responsibility for any libel lawsuits.
Speaking of which ...
This book is a *complete* work of fiction. Names, characters, places, opinions, dreams, dates, impressions, monologues about a certain New York City basketball team, emotional trauma, statistics, and predictions are products of the author's imagination and/or are symptoms of mental illness. We are not in the business of accepting responsibility for anything and will deny we actually made this book and blame Julius Randle at every turn.

First Edition:10 19 33 34 6 11 1973
ISBN: 978-0-9997138-8-4
LOC: 2021930211

Design, Layout, and Edits: Ezhno Martín
Cover: Grant Whipple

For Erica Fischer, Jim Moore, James Moore, Sharon Moore,
Nelson Algren and Richard Linklater

In Honor of friends and family in & around Houston and
Texas . . . and beyond.

Inspired by Hank Anderson *(1980-2015)*

"Drink 'Till We're Gone"

Life is short

in spite of your plans
so tell the girls they're pretty while you can.
One day they're gone
and all you got left is
some empty bottles and an old country song
that plays on and on.

I wasted my time with these cigarettes
and these ashes all I've got left.
Wash this old town
nothing's left for me
washed down stream into the sea.
This big ol' river will kill us in time
'till then we'll drink its weight
in cheap beer and wine.
We can drink just as fast as the river is strong
and we'll drink 'till we're gone.

We'll drink 'till we're gone.

— **Lucero**

THE PHALANX OF HOUSTON

a Novel
Walter Moore

THURSDAY NIGHT

After a brief stop-off with friends in Austin, I landed in the Houston Greyhound bus terminal — started walking from that downtown hub of hedonism and all things awry towards the Montrose neighborhood, stopped for a beer at a Midtown bar, of the kind Houston contains so many of: converted garages with open-air doors and large windows, a broad wooden patio in front. Bar inside but mostly patrons outside. One beer turned into a few: a few beers converted into some bad shots of well bourbon, and in the parking lot, a quiet woman in a green dress along with two younger guys were walking away; two midtown bros that put on khaki shorts and casual button-downs after work, probably in downtown offices for big oil and gas.

They both had on boat shoes even though there was no natural water for miles.

I was at a picnic table by myself next to the exit. "Obama is a Muslim. He won't touch Iran," said one of them. The woman next to them in the green dress didn't say anything, just finished her bottle of beer.

"Or at least a Muslim sympathizer," the other one, a pudgy one, said. I am not a political person, not often, but the clash of Austin residue and this yuppie bar, the long Greyhound ride, the wretched terminal with its fake pills and used batteries and war-torn vaginas, my vulnerable and heightened nervous system that felt outside my body, my return to the humid beast exacerbated by this (mis)information:

The Phalanx was dead.

I corrected him as I stood up towards the exit sidewalk: "He's not a Muslim, you motherfucker." The roly-poly took a step in retreat, but this other one with a more utilized gym membership did not miss a beat, leaned in.

"Just head back inside, buddy," he keened. I knew his kind, the flimsy talk of a card house.

"You ignorant fuck," I said.

"What did you say?" He smirked. "That's a nice beard you got, buddy."

"Let me take a picture of that beard," the other one said from a safe distance, raising his smartphone.

"What are you, some kind of liberal snowflake?" asked the first one.

The night was down so I braced myself. There was no moon, Baby Jesus in bed unattended. And ignorance and technology: I hate cellular phones, don't own one nor a computer or a television or anything; so I hit the guy, slightly awkward, side of his face. "Independent," I said.

He was a bit drunk himself, took a retaliatory swing, but his arm was slow, a languid noodle not prepared for confrontation of the physically intimate kind.

His hours at the posh gym hadn't readied him.

I hit him again, in the ear. The blood sudden and lavish. The roly-poly started to scream as he pointed with his baby computer. The collared gym rat started to yell. They made noises in tandem with increasing enthusiasms — and amid the *fuck you's* and *you asshole's*, a few of their coughs and sweats, a *this is all on camera buddy you've done it now!* — I couldn't help but think about The Phalanx, how he would have navigated this episode with more justification and grace — how his provocation for violence always seemed smoothly earned, like the movies; right and wrong pronounced; clear visions of the celebrated hero in the idealistic minds of the audience members.

And then the woman in the green dress smashed her bottle on the side of my head.

Going down to the curb, I thought, and now think, about my history of bad timing and ambivalence . . . as a couple of cops came over, as the bro got a stack of napkins for his bleeding ear, as the roly-poly told the story in already overblown embellishment. He gestured wildly to the cops and to the people on that night patio.
With blood coming down the side of my face — as the two bros took photographs of one another, as my nerves were shot — I sat down on that curb cursing Houston and pitying and glorifying The Phalanx.
As they arrested me, the handcuffs felt rigid and heavy, more uncomfortable than painful. This type of thing had happened before, a stale routine by that time.

And that woman in the green dress was nowhere

to be found, having tiptoed away into the arms of a nicer night. Into the arms of more peaceful strangers.

But I do remember liking her dress.

With the other reeling deviants going through their rituals in the downtown jail, people in uniforms stripped me down, took photographs of my tattoos, shuffled me through rooms and an elevator and stairs, asked me many questions, and put me in a cell with two other men.

More dehydrated than drunk, I was exhausted and overheated . . . numb to the mechanisms of this worn-down though sterile building — my mind an extension of a grey and ringing tunnel of fatigued disorientation, but my two cellmates spoke to each other as if they were at a midday horserace, pleasantly goosed on good gin and sunshine.

"My woman is a panty dropper."
"I hear that. Shit."
"A fine piece."
"You got it."

For maybe an hour I slept, but a man in another cell kept crying out for the authorities, any of the manmade gods to nurse him.

"*Iyeeeeeeeee!* ... *help me!* ... *thaluuuuuuump!* ...
Christ! ... *iyeeeeeeeeee!* ... *God!* ... *gaaaaaaaawhd!*"

This went on for hours — the animal screeches and mortal pleads. No one in charge seemed to care, but after a season we heard: "Yo, this man needs some help! I think this motherfucker is dead!" There was a faint alarm, staff-members rushed in, and a mound of limp flesh on a stretcher was taken past us in a blur of excretion and stench.

"Yo, man, this shit ain't right!" someone yelled. One of my roommates just murmured: "*Mmmm. Humph.*" One of the horses had collapsed. This was nothing new for them, though their gin had worn off.

Due to bureaucratized regulation, they corralled us into a holding cell, thirty tight in a room; I sat on the faded linoleum against a wall, arms wrapped around my knees. Some not-right goon pointed at me. "I am going to kill you, motherfucker! I'm a bad man!"

I learned later the man crying out in that cell had experienced a series of seizures and died.

The emptiness, apparent now with the stopping of a heart, was in the threats — also in those walls, in the city itself that had been constructed on cheap lumber and generous loan applications, on the profits of this downtown jail and the mistakes of the other two million plus bodies landlocked and purgatoried slightly below sea level in the new city that was once a swamp. On the sinister phone call I made, on the bail bondsman I would pay to get me out of there — all of it an unnoticed slot machine for the dispossessed and closed in.

All of it on the wrong side of a billboard.

Houston, of course, within its confines, has few limits.

FRIDAY AFTERNOON/EVENING

"They say you can't step into the same river twice, boy. But my fucking foot sure still looks the same."

— **Boyd Leonard,** *drunk.*

I could see Leonard's duplex from a half block down, its peeling façade a depreciation of any good man or woman's senses.

Lawn needed mowing, I assumed at least one utility had not been paid. My guess was the gas, which was ironic yet fitting.

Some empty Budweiser cans were on the modest rectangle slab of a porch, proffered aluminum in a bush. I remember Leonard one time after drinking a Bud Light: "Goddamnit, Patsy, why do you buy this goddamn nothin' beer!"

Patsy, still with him at that time, was not impressed: "Well, hell. You could use a little more water in your piss!"

His side of the well-worn rental 'plex had a modest red Texas star painted on the outside below a large front window, a window that looked like it had been slashed with a machete in a too dark night — the inside dust-ridden mini-blinds, also nearly torn in two, sagged lamely.

Below the window crooked on top of forgotten bushes in the front lawn was an old wooden canoe, its color greener than the grass, one solid oar resting on top.

These residences on this gentrified street in this neighborhood diverse in type and size were indications of the status of the owners and tenants — from gates nearly pearly to trash piles in between red stars and beer cans and missing oars.

Leonard's door was open, the place looked as if all the corpses and women had left the building, leaving only shit and debris for the first world to smell the spoiled soil that was the air. Ashtrays proper and makeshift wondered what their simple composites had bargained for. Glass and metal as cast-off soldiers, a cracked CD case, Townes Van Zandt's album *Flying Shoes* on the ground, the case the best treated item amid the wreckage of an alcoholic with occasional psychotic tendencies.

I saw the bastard on the couch, in his underwear. He had been overserved, his belly an overcharged muscle exploding away from the chest — fat and rock supporting the tortured organs, Leonard snoring, and dying in his sleep in front of me.

Sleep is not peaceful if the fiends vie for your attention like cheerleaders towards the quarterback in a bad movie.

I poked Leonard hard in the neck. He didn't wake. Located a CD called *Half Nelson*, a compilation of Willie Nelson duets, turned it up on the boom box, "Pancho and Lefty" amped to a painful afternoon hangover volume. Leonard shifted into the couch, an adjustment of his secondhand womb.

> *The desert's quiet*
> *Cleveland's cold*

... standing over him, I noticed that red face, the rosacea — silver hair, yellow toenails from almost five decades of smoking, the poses of a long-ago Texas Hill Country poor kid.

> *They only let him go so long*
> *out of kindness I suppose*

"Leonard!"

"Shit!" He jerked to. I turned Willie off. "Shit, boy. How did you get in here?"

"Unlocked." He let out heavy breath, gauged me

through fog. Though he was a misfortunate, his eyes still held wherewithal, a quick mind beyond the endless closing times of his soul. "Nice canoe you got there on the front lawn. Get much use?"

"Shit, no. Not yet." He massaged his navel and widened his eyes. "Where you coming from?"

"Was just in Austin for a few days. Got in last night. Been in Vermont. Took the Greyhound here . . . to this mess."

He got up to his cluttered kitchen to make coffee, lit a cigarette, looked at me strange. "What brings you after so long?"

"The Phalanx."

"Marius? How is that boy?"

"The Phalanx died." He sighed, looked out the window to nothing — to Montrose.

"How then?"

"Not sure. They found his body at his condo week back. His mom tracked me down, called the place I work . . . well, used to work now I guess."

"How is Victoria? She was always a fine-lookin' woman."

"I don't think she leaves her house much — said maybe he died of an overdose, not sure."

He puckered his mouth — "strange lives you boys lead" — and his accent was slow thick Texan, a crawling boom that stressed the first syllable of words, took unlikely pauses . . . had time and spaces in sentences for unhurried contemplation. "You don't look so good, Bjorn."

"I say the same for you."

"Was he playing soccer?

"Yeah, he was still playing soccer."

"Well . . . I'll be." He motioned for the outside world with his oversized hand.

I expressed some of the details to Leonard about my night and morning hours before. He was bothered but not that surprised. He'd had his jail-time detours himself, on Bandera stony lonesome sawdust and otherwise. Leonard had spent nearly a year in the Navy (we never got the full story of why he was discharged, but we can guess); he'd worked many jobs with his hands as a younger man, but primarily, alongside being a good timer and malcontent, he had worked outside as a maintenance man of generators and pumps and filter systems on natural gas plants.

Natural gas, on/off — from his no-nothin' and have-nothing Hill Country days to settling in Houston about 30 years ago, to working sporadically under Texas suns for multinational oil and gas, he'd had over twenty jobs my count but kept quitting and getting let go, letting go — for acting irrational towards younger bosses than himself, for being too drunk, hungover, for more general insubordination. He was smart enough and good with his hands when he wanted to be, which had kept him in it and going on occasions, but he did not possess the requisite constitution for team building. He was charming at the first but didn't fit in with people enough over a long term, and his own digressions had positioned him in strictures of the disreputable sort. He had an off-the-cuff penchant for dancing with prostitutes at bars for one.

"Isn't this a cock fuck 'em. I would call you the prodigal son, but as I recall you haven't done shit. You need to keep your nose clean, Bjorn."

"Sure."

"Why didn't you call me to come bail you out?"

"Don't have your number. Don't have a phone."

"And Obama *is* a Muslim sympathizer."

"If sympathizer you mean he doesn't outright hate Muslims."

"Shit, boy, you lose a family member or some limbs to some lunatic with a cheap bomb rig strapped to his chest, you see how much sympathy you have."

"I don't see you suffering from any terrorist attacks."

"That's right . . . hmph . . . you say that *now* . . . you just wait until it hits you in the dickem'. You care then."

"Right."

"Remember you're talking to a veteran."

"Hardly. You never left the country. How did you avoid Vietnam anyway?"

He added bourbon to his coffee. "War practically over by then . . . but let's just say they best needed me to guard the nation." *Naaay-shun.*

I sat down on the couch as a gesture to end this ridiculous thread.

"So you was just in Austin, huh?"

"Couple days."

"As if all the fruits and nuts in California ain't bad enough."

"Better than this shithole."

"Hmph . . . at least the shit looks like shit around here. Not like shit disguised as peacocks."

"Yet you live in the most progressive neighborhood in the city."

He snorted. "*Pro-gressive?* Close proximity to nearly unlimited watering holes."

"High rent now too I imagine."

"Nah, the landlord's an old timer. Known him for years. Charges me a respectable rate on account of an understanding."

"Yeah?"

"Let's just say I don't judge his affinities for drink and questionable women and occasionally dressing like the prom queen."

"Seems you get along with peacocks just fine," I said.

He swatted at the remark, turned to face me square. "So, Marius is dead?" he asked.

"Bar crawl tonight in his honor. Service on Sunday."

"Let's get a good drink now then, boy." After taking a swig, he looked down into his now barren coffee cup, held at an angle.

"Put on some pants . . . any news from Patsy?"

"Still on the cruise ship I 'spose." Patsy would come back for a time now and again, but she had left Leonard's house and life more permanently about a decade ago. The nights had gotten too deranged on both ends, so she drifted. As would I.

"You not working these days?"

"Laid off couple weeks back. Petroleum in the shitter again."

"Could I get one of those?"

Leonard handed me a cigarette, lit it for me. The inhaled smoke felt like oxygen.

He was, after all, my father.

One Note

This only explains my immediate family, and only partly at that. My extended family story is more complicated and elusive.

Quick rundown though: Patsy was an only child in Texas City, and her folks died when she was a teenager not long before she hitched up with Leonard in Galveston right after he got discharged. Leonard's father was in and out of (mostly in) prison for writing hot checks and other perpetual petty bullshit around the Hill Country. His mother heard voices and was in the hospital, so Leonard and his eight siblings grew up in and out of boys and girls' homes and at relatives' houses when they had the means to take them in. His older brother Burn, who I've only met once, is an uncertified taxidermist who lives in a house in Fredericksburg with eleven cats and six dogs, with a wife and ex-wife (two sisters). Occasionally Burn scoops up roadkill and stuffs it to make ends.

Leonard's other brothers and sisters are scattered around Medina and Kerrville and Bandera and San Antonio and other parts of Texas. When I was about eight years old I got stuck talking to his uncle, my great uncle. This man's story is ludicrous. When he was about twenty, he and some other guy held up a gas station in the middle of California, ran out and pulled a gun on an old trucker; the trucker proceeded to keel over out of shock, and this great-uncle of mine was convicted of manslaughter and spent 22 years in prison.

Alone with him one afternoon at a kitchen
table when I was about eight, he told me shitty
stories about prison and how I should never go.
Life lesson. Maybe I was too young to let that one
sink in. Leonard's oldest brother Bert is dead now
but he lived in Houston for many years, on the
north side of town, and worked for the telephone
company. His wife lives with their daughter in
Tyler. His son, Buddy, lives in Temple, Texas, and
paints houses. Leonard's younger brother Beau-
Tom has been married seven times to four women
(all dead), and he lives by himself now in Hondo.

Beau-Tom has seven kids and 17 grandkids
scattered around Texas. I can barely keep up but
here's a short rundown of them: an evangelical
preacher in Boerne, a woman who works in a
liquor store in Ft. Worth, a man who works as a
custodial engineer in Beaumont . . . another cousin
who works at a pawn shop in Corpus; others who
are addicted to meth, in jail, one chasing speed
mules and doing God knows what in Amarillo,
and at least one grandkid who is homeless. That
little beautiful gutterpunk plays the guitar and
sometimes pounds a bucket on the side of the
street in San Marcos for cash. Last time I saw
him he said Beau-Tom could go fuck himself, then
proceeded to tell me a story about this dude he
knew at Whataburger who liked to milk his third
nipple for late-night drive-thru customers. Say
what you want, but my family members like to tell
jokes and stories, and they all like to laugh and
have a good time, far as I know.

Granted no one went to college, or at least no one
has graduated. No one has much money, far as I
know either. Leonard's middle sister Bet Pearl (now
deceased) has a bunch of kids and grandkids too.
Her daughter was a prostitute and meth addict,
now rehabilitated I heard; her son is a security

guard in Bastrop who has a conman for a son, I'm sorry to say; though he seemed like a really nice guy when I met him. Course he took my money.

Others include a truck driver, construction workers, a line cook at a Tex-Mex restaurant in Buda, and one in jail outside Bryan-College Station, last I checked. ALL Republicans; all raised Church of Christ with a love of the 2nd Amendment, Jesus, and the Dallas Cowboys.

Many of them have died before the age of 60.

Consequently, in response, I am Independent, bitter, and have a complicated relationship with God; I do not own a gun. Only like to punch people in the face on occasion.

We all like to get fucked up.

So . . . yes — divorces, domestic violence, addiction, insanity, and all-star Texas-American dysfunction. One story from a while back of my nine-year-old cousin hiding in a closet while her parents were fighting: Her father hit her mother, her mother pulled a handgun on her father, and this kid came out of the closet and pulled a handgun on both of her parents to get them to stop the nonsense. Only thing is the parents were already post-fight fornicating on the carpet. No shots were fired. That nine-year-old just dropped the gun and went to her room, leaving her parents. She's now a teenager and works and lives at an assisted living home in San Antonio, all bills paid. She seems like a nice person.

This is my extended family, give/take on Leonard's side. I don't know them well and do not see them very often at all. They all live in Texas, and I'm the only one who has lived outside the state, far as I know — except that great-uncle who held up that old trucker; he was in Bakersfield drifting around when that happened and his prison time was in California; naturally, he hates California and said he will never go back to the land of "fruits and nuts" (a phrase my family likes to repeat).

I guess I can't blame him too much. He passed away a few years ago of natural causes. Many of these relatives call me a "Yankee" though they don't really know me. (I've never been out of the country, except Mexico and Canada briefly). We are *not* the Brady Bunch nor Duck Dynasty nor any of that other shit people watch on TV. Just a bunch of disconnected dreams and dead ends and sober and drunk realities under various Texas skies. Good people trying to do the best they can.

Amen.

Don't try to remember these details. The point is I don't know these other family members well enough to write at length about them. Maybe one day if I ever leave these Colorado mountains and move back to Texas and spend more time with them.

I know they like a good yarn.

As of now, they only serve as a footnote here for this other story.

So I left Houston at seventeen, almost eighteen, not yet anything, but enough hair on the scrote. Nothing no longer made sense, but something did — call it conditioning for change and drifting. Patsy, our matriarch, had left. I had no other family in the city, and the relatives I barely knew were scattered around the state and had enough problems of their own.

Leonard and I'd constantly moved in and out of rental apartments within blocks of one another. School seemed irrational: the apathetic teachers, the institution of needless busywork, the soccer coach who had kicked me off the team my senior year for having long hair.

It was just me and Leonard then, and we didn't make very good drinking partners. His wife's departure mangled with the stressors of his shifting jobs and constant debt had left him addling, despising the conditions of his routine: go to work, come home, halfway pay your bills, drink. Leonard's bottle kissing always resembled that of any pious alcoholic for the first few hours. He would get jovial, affectionate, long-winded with his storytelling and monologues, but whereas a typical alcoholic might get angry before passing out, Leonard would push through with his superior metabolism. His anger would turn to mixed mirage, of his mind's haunted specters of his Hill Country past and his current drone, of a boss and co-workers and larger society who were evil in his mind's eye — to violent indignation and righteousness of the most internally and physically destructive kind — to wanting just to have a good old time and hope to temporarily forget his problems.

He howled, he punched me, he broke everything. He fought me, sometimes while I was asleep. He was hardly six foot but carried himself, especially while drunk, as if he were much larger.

But I was still growing, and this behavior could not keep.

After sleeping on a few couches, I left Houston — found myself in Oklahoma City, that buckle of hypocritical deliverance, bussing tables at a restaurant and living with two other employees in a small house north of town.

Not long after, The Phalanx rode up to see me.

The Phalanx, or Marius Malanx, my closest friend, had a way about him — a comforting grin and this soft-spoken elocution yet twitchy physical velocity could both ease and enliven a scene, help you momentarily believe your disappointments were needless.

We stayed up drinking cheap beers and bourbon out of bottles one night, listening to music in the living room. One of Oklahoma's famous twister tornado storms was about to come — an alert and whirring siren via Doppler had advised us to find a basement or windowless room, but we didn't mind.

In that tract '50s-style house, in the front outside rested a six-by-six block of cement I called *the capsule*. A southern rock opera protested from a roommate's stereo just inside the front door, and I and The Phalanx sat on the capsule as we watched the shifting colors of the storm clouds dictated by the approaching tornado. It began to rain, and the Oklahoma winds took hold of the surrounding red dirt plains and its inhabitants, the winds old hat to them but exciting to us.

"How long are you going to stay in Oklahoma?" he asked me.

"Not forever. I plan on picking up not before too long."

"You think you might come back to Houston?"

"Probably not. Too much baggage there. I can't imagine growing old there." He laughed, poured bourbon into a glass formerly used for jam.

"You're already old, Bjorn. You talk like a crotched grandpa. Think the world's run its course."

"You know what I mean. Who wants to have a life in that place? It's a damn swamp. No one could live there until they invented air conditioning. Who wants to live in a city that runs on air conditioning?"

"It's good enough there. The weather makes people come together." He tugged on his blond beard. "You could live somewhere in Houston, never run the a.c. You can sweat it out all day long if you want to."

"That would be fine, but I no longer want to sweat it out in my car while I'm stuck in that traffic."

"It's not like Oklahoma is beautiful. There's a reason the Trail of Tears ended here. Let me tell you something. Every place has its less desirables. Like a person."

"You telling me you are going to impregnate Houston, marry it sometime soon?"

He laughed that great laugh with full-bodied grin.

"No. I've accepted that offer to play for the University of Denver. Going to make a go of that."

"Damn." I nodded. "College soccer in Colorado. Good for you."

The rain picked up, wind nudging our cross-legged postures; we were shirtless, music loud, and we could see the funnel of condensation beyond the rooftops. Rumbling distant sounds of the spiraling vortex: faint siren, booms of what resembled a freight train or rushing rapids, maybe a waterfall or a nearby jet engine — a whooshing roar. There in tornado alley, that cyclone, possibly an F-4, looked like a tree-shaped vessel of wind mostly dark and grey with specks of pink from the red dirt and debris. Those post-WWII houses, better than trailer homes but susceptible to clockwise motion and the signaled violence of the thing, as the base of it started to widen and I could smell the renewal of the ominous wedge. Over those rooftops I gleaned the natural hologram of a puffed-up snake's head, and we cheered to it, clinked to it, yelled:

"Come and take it!"

"Come and take us, you bastard!" I drank some beer from a bottle, espoused to The Phalanx: "You sure you don't want to go back inside, before you get injured, you soccer pussy?!"

"I was worried about those pretty dish-scrubbing hands of yours!"

We stayed out there on the capsule through the pink storm and encroaching darkness, drunk on the fruits of the near black cosmos and friendship, until the ascending sun finally presented its orange breast, a cherry on top of a junk pile.

We had not owned the night, but we were not much afraid of it neither.

"I'll ask you again, Leonard: Why is there an unused canoe in your front yard?"

"Shit, you never know when this place gets flooded. Parts of this town below sea level. Never know when you're going to need a boat."

"Logical," I said as Leonard and I began to walk through the neighborhood, sweating among the buildings and hipsters.

He stopped to sit on a bench, catch his breath. "This neighborhood used to actually have homosexuals — now it's filled with I don't know what. Bunch of squirrely types in tight pants."

"Seems there's still an LGBTQ presence . . . just more money now," I said.

"I liked it better with the gays. There weren't a

bunch of idiots with outside influence making so many eye-sore investments."

"There you go again. Never knew you were so progressive."

"Shit. Progressive nothin'. It don't take a communist to know what's good for people living in a neighborhood. Now, I don't need all those gays and hippies necessarily, but a man needs his local ambience." He stressed the first syllable in his slow idiosyncratic pronunciation: *alm-be-awnse*.

"Very progressive. You've come a long way since the Hill Country, old man."

"Shit. See that McDonald's. That Starbucks — those aren't establishments: *eye-sores*. Just like the crap condos. They are so adamant." He pronounced this last word *adda-mant*.

"Maybe you should start your own business," I said.

"Hmph . . . barely got enough money for a stand to sell my piss out of a jar."

We settled at a bar-restaurant across the street from the private Menil Museum and its louvered roof, that nice adjacent park with its cypress and oak trees and surrounding bungalows of gray — teenagers smoking and lounging in the grass, off West Alabama Street to Mandell to West Main Street: a place called the Seedy Café with its culinary fusion of affordable eats.

Positioning ourselves in one of Seedy's cramped booths along the side wall, Leonard, though possessing too much girth for casual booth dining, looked rejuvenated with the emergent possibility of liquids.

"Haven't heard from you in a time. Where you been again?"

"Vermont for over a year now. Bartending mostly. Living in staff housing at this resort hotel in the mountains."

"*Ver-mont.* Very nice. Shit, boy, livin' low rent in some *re-zort* seems like a commie *'rangement* you picked up. I know as well as anybody being born drifter poor in this country like being born with one leg. A person can hop around on that leg, maybe get some income. Don't get me wrong, *some people* maybe need wooden legs given to them by the all-American government, other people can work and buy that leg for themselves — but not every one-legged son-of-a-bitch needs to be handed a wooden leg for free."

"Your powers of analogy astound me. You're not even drunk yet I don't think."

"*Analogy?* You talk as if you went to college, but as far as I can tell you're just a brokedick barback living in free housing."

"Bartender. I read a lot of paperbacks." A pop-punk song started playing. "Besides, don't act like all legs are the same. And my housing's not free."

"All legs are the same, boy. It's just that the majority of this country ain't but got one leg. But every leg hops around like it's bare-toed in chickenshit just the same. Some just like the shit more than others, thinks it's warm and comforting on their members." He pointed his fat finger at me. "Thing is, I think you like twiddlin' the chickenshit a little too much."

I started to laugh.

This guy, this old man who comprised half my DNA baffled me, but I knew he wasn't all wrong — even truthfulness veiled in eccentric rationale if you could wade through his own chickenshit.

"Well, you here now." He scrunched his face in a pucker. "Came back for the funeral, huh? We was worried about you."

I wondered who was the *we* he was referring to. "Were you."

"What's it been? Few years since we seen you last?"

"Not much to come back for I guess."

"You're too young to be bitter, boy. I don't understand."

"Are you out of your mind?" He looked at me toughly, trying to read me. I wondered if he read the several Houston addresses rifling my mind. "Before I left here for good, we had just lived in half a dozen apartments in four years because you kept losing jobs. We kept moving, a few blocks at a time. Patsy had left, and you were a psychotic mess."

"Why do you call your mother by her first name?"

"Because I've only seen her once in a few years. Because she left. She left me with you, man."

"Well?"

"For fuck sake. You were psychotic. *Are psychotic* still, far as I can tell. All the late-night rants, the bizarre behavior. And on special occasions you hit me in my fucking sleep." I looked away to the fake black leather of the adjacent booth and its missing button, to the black tinted windows of the place — to a sign for *drag brunch on sunday*, to a framed velvet photo of Yoda — vinyl album covers on walls (Charlie Pride, James Taylor, Joni Mitchell, Jonny Matthis), old beer posters (the band Modest Mouse playing through speakers), a lit-up sign that said

I love you this much
< >

... along with the glow of a neon Winston cigarette clock. I took a drink from my Lone Star tall boy, and looking up noticed the rafters covered with insulation that looked like asbestos ... and I sighed because these combinations made little sense ... or too much sense. I looked again at Leonard. "It got to where I couldn't go to sleep. Don't you remember when I knocked you out not long before I left for good? Broke my hand on your forehead?"

"I don't remember that, but you've told me about it. We can't change the past, Bjorn. Wish I could."

He actually looked hurt, even sensitive to it all, but I knew he didn't possess the emotional capacity to completely empathize.

I noticed a fish bowl filled with flowers and a neon light that said

Montrose, TX.

"Anyway . . . that shit stays with you. And I don't like coming back to this shithole to be reminded of it at all."

"It is a swamp," he agreed.

The waiter came over with our beers, along with V8 juice for Leonard with a stick of celery on the side. He liked to combine the juice and beer himself rather than have the bartender do it, making what is called in cocktail parlance a Red Eye. He loved drinking Red Eyes during the day; with the V8, it's the closest he ever comes to eating a salad, and the Seedy Café with its XMas lights and flea market finds on the walls, its perky waiters, its line cooks with their war stories and bad tattoos actually from prison, was his kind of fine dining. "I see they've added hummus to the menu," he said. *Hoom-us.* "And of course there's chicken fried steak. Damn good breakfast here."

"I've been here before with you. Years ago."

"Well, then."

He mixed the juice with the beer, bit off half the celery and gulped the Red Eye like a newly rescued P.O.W., and I had to ask: "When are you going to stop all this? Why don't you get some help?"

"Things ain't as bad as they was." He swirled his now empty drink. "I went to a head doctor one time. He said it was okay to self-medicate."

"Some doctor. That's just the sort of opinion you need."

"I got *your* opinion, all right . . . nah . . . things aren't that bad. I'm an old man now, boy. I don't do all that anymore."

"I can tell by the V8."

"You are a puritanical one. Just a hangover. Some hangovers. But I ain't angry. Not greedy no more either." He sounded sincere about this.

And he pointed a spoon at me, closed one eye: "You just got out of jail. You don't much have the right to tell me nothin'."

We changed the subject and Leonard went off on petroleum, how the cyclical and fickle nature of the industry bred instability, especially in the minds and hearts of the plant workers. He enjoyed an opportunity for a good monologue about natural gas. I only half listened because I had heard all of it before — about the hierarchy of engineers and superintendants and managers and operators, down through the maintenance men and laborers like himself. And I felt sorry for him. Some good in that heart of his. Just never had a chance for health, for a functional life. From small-town Texas with eight siblings who were mostly abandoned and always poor as shit, to getting out, to the Gulf of Mexico, to briefly serving in the military, to marrying Patsy when she was still in high school — to his many jobs and the company man bullshit he hated. He never had much of a chance. His generation of men never got to openly feel sorry for themselves I don't think. Never were allowed to outwardly feel in a truthful way. I didn't completely blame him, but I couldn't completely blame myself much either for being a mess. *Blame.* Not a precise application wherein there's a generations'-long hand-me-down history of delusion and dysfunction. Like a gunshot. You can't blame the bullet.

You can't *fully* blame a bullet for its trajectory nor the type of metal it's been ordained.

I was only a kid in Houston, and nearly a decade later I was still grappling with my own stunted and latent emotional maturity. I had found ways to remember and forget. This *return* wasn't exactly about healing. It was about acceptance of that shitty movie in my head, the realization I had snuck into a violent porn video at an early age. I should never have been on that set, in that theatre, in that room, in that *space* to begin with, but now with added age I was attempting to better understand all of it.

I thought about The Phalanx too, how he was a good friend to me — on that high school soccer team but mostly outside of that. He was one of the best players in the city and the state even then, an athletic freak and stand-out force. I was a decent player, respectable for that type of team, but that wasn't why The Phalanx and I were friends. While my response was typically downcast, the lame stitching of tired wounds, The Phalanx kept it light. He was earnest and gregarious yet soft-spoken (which meant you'd have to lean in close), and he smiled and laughed a lot — making for a damn charming combo; but if you knew him his formative years had not been wonderful either, aside from the athletic success. His father died on a motorcycle when The Phalanx was in middle school, and Marius "The Phalanx" Malanx seemed to embody his dad's renegade streak with his very own kind of maverick risk-taking. And his mother had a number of phobias — wouldn't leave the house for sometimes weeks at a time, even though, as Leonard says, she was good lookin'.

No, The Phalanx was that rare type of friend that understood. We didn't have to talk much. The understanding was there, and we also both liked to drink and smoke and rarely refuse much of anything offered. We liked to play pool or shuffleboard and put money into local jukeboxes. And he came out to see me everywhere I've lived. Oklahoma, Austin, Indiana, Brooklyn, Providence in Rhode Island, the mountains of Vermont — the notches of my aimless north and eastern migration.

Every time we spoke, we mentioned finding a way to live in the same city. Just not Houston. The beginning of the place had to be clean, or so I always thought.

I looked across the table at Leonard as he talked. He puffed on an electronic cigarette because you couldn't smoke otherwise indoors. Beneath that vapor and rosacea and bluster, I saw myself a bit — a child with self-doubts. Fearful that the world may punch you in your sleep, that a friend would never visit you again, even as a twister attempted to rip the rooftops off the houses of broken families. Even as your car breaks down ninety miles south of Denver and you've forgotten which way is home.

Stopping my train too, Leonard interrupted his long-winded discourse with a grunt and a flick of his cylinder in disregard: "This e-cigarette is a poor substitute," he said, doubly displeased with his Red Eye drained long gone. "Can't feel nothin' with this thing."

The waiter approached us. "Sir, you can't smoke e-cigarettes inside here."

"Shit." Leonard blew out a cloud. "Just vapors."

I finished my beer and threw some cash on the table. "I'm not hungry. Let's move along."

Leonard threw my cash back at me. "This is mine." I threw the cash back at him and he then crammed the bills in my front shirt pocket. "No need to mouthfuck a gift horse, boy."

The Seedy was stagnant, Leonard was ready for outside air, as was I, and the motions of the city and favored neighborhood were waiving us forward, calling for reprieve. "Let's put our toes in some shit," I said, "find you another leg."

"Peacock," he said, noticing a gaunt, bearded stranger in tight black leather pants dead of summer across the street. "Worse than squirrelly."

#3

At that time, Leonard's life lessons to me had long been moribund, but I at least attempted to convey some decency towards him, with one listening ear, with the other ear quietly beckoning the road's advices of fatherly vagabonds.

"Always know a man's credentials."

He said this after having relayed a story from when he was sixteen at a honky-tonk in Bandera, Texas — a hill country roughneck cowboy town, early 1970s.

That Friday night of the pub crawl in Montrose, before we had walked into a bar called the Lotus Tree, Leonard told me this story as a lesson in keeping one's nose clean before entering any drinking establishment. Blowing smoke into the hot wet air, he puffed his body out, looked at me sideways to make sure I had been paying attention.

The story entailed the teenaged Leonard talking big at the bar to some clean-cut adult with a flat-top haircut, maybe late twenties. The dispute consisted of a spilled beer and a misunderstanding in Leonard's eyes, which amid the tension and Leonard's misguided sophomoric bravado, he had asked the keen gentlemen if he would like to step outside.

As you do.

As one gentleman does.

This man in particular then proceeded to kick the shit out of him.

Leonard pointed to a small nearly unnoticeable scar above his right brow. "Was just punching air while he knocked me around like a frozen meat carcass." This guy had been a boxer in the United States military, with a winning record reportedly. His fists were like irons.

"Lyke eye earns," he said it. Leonard told me this man was a golden gloves champion, but I didn't believe that. I chose to believe he was just a strong arm in the military.

Or maybe just a strong arm.

"And what I learned: Always know a man's credentials."

"What the fuck does that mean, Leonard? How are you supposed to know someone's credentials every time you get into a confrontation with them?"

"I'm just saying, you should always know what you are getting into."

"But we don't always know what we are getting into. That's the problem usually. If we did, we wouldn't fuck up as much as we do."

He exhaled a sigh, ashed downward. "Boy, you exhaust me."

In that Lotus Tree bar for the wake and pub crawl, abreast of the pinball machines, scattered neon lights and modest row of cans of local beers on display, I noticed the enlarged memorial poster-sized photograph of The Phalanx — capturing his genial grin and that stupid haircut, which reminded me of his unconventional approach to his career.

After three years in Denver, The Phalanx was drafted as a forward late in the last round by the professional team in Houston — partially because two of the organization's player development coaches knew him, vouched for his at-times sudden bursts of speed and power with that unorthodox left foot of his. Perhaps they knew exactly what he would become, that he would never be a legitimate starter as a professional; he liked a good time at night with his substances, his recreational experiments on the metabolizing body a fixture — he was too wild and too inconsistently skilled for ninety minutes of reliable play, but they did know, as I had long realized, that with time he could turn into a viable super-sub with appropriately timed effectiveness late in games. Which he had become and displayed more recently with newfangled fanfare.

After being drafted late, he was demoted for a few seasons to the team's lower squad in San Antonio, playing there often with success. He finally made the senior squad, albeit barely, that season before his death, and for the rest of his eternal soccer life, he will have logged eighty minutes as a major league professional, scoring only one goal. But in the typical Phalanx style that lone goal was a goddamned thing of beauty. He came on around the sixtieth minute in a home game against Kansas City. In the 87th minute, he took a long running pass down the left flank, an adept descending first touch around three defenders and inward to the eighteen, corner of the box, and shot the ball with a violence and curling miraculous precision past the keeper, top left corner/upper ninety. It was his manic burst, a bit of luck, and that left foot that had won the game.

Where we come from, he had made it — leaving the rest of us rubes to only marvel at this man in 2D who had done something notable on the screen and in paper. The only documented figure of stature many of us had actually known in the flesh too, from our forgettable pasts to our projected unremarkable futures.

That glorious shot garnered footage on lower-rung sports shows and found its way into the sports sections of Houston newspapers. The local boy had done good. Plus, that haircut was perfect for a snapshot and soundbite:

Marius Malanx. Half Man. Half Crazy.

He had half of a faux-hawk on one side of his head's top. The other side was completely shaven to the skull. He also wore a long blond beard, but the opposite side of his face and chin from the crown of his head's barren side was shaved, making for a symmetrical hairstyle of the most ridiculous kind. I remember when The Phalanx got that asshat haircut — the *beard hawk* as he called it. Half beard: Half hawk. Crazy in front, stupid in back.

We were in Brooklyn, in Greenpoint. He had come back from a Polish barber with it. Greenpoint was generally Eastern European, still predominately Polish back then.

Maybe it was the artists and pretenders in the newly gentrified neighborhood that had inspired such a misstep, but he felt good and creative about the haircut. Saw it as his signature.

"What the fuck is that supposed to be?" I asked, pointing to his head and face.

He smiled. "I need a hook, my friend. A way to be remembered by."

"You think you're going to be the Denis Rodman of American soccer or some shit?"

"That wouldn't be the worst thing in the world. It's like a mullet but sideways. A little bit of something for everybody."

And he was right.

People loved the hair. It's amazing how a haircut makes such simple palpable sense for the media and the fans. The Phalanx was memorable, the

image molded in the collective pop-cultural
consciousness, or at least in the *local* consciousness,
rather firmly in this basic fashion. People held up
placards: *Release The Phalanx! Half Man, Half
Crazy!* They would chant for him, cheer for him,
while he stayed firmly planted on the bench. The
public perception being he was a wild beast that
needed to be released, his tyranny let loose to the
mercy of the opposing players.

And he was from Houston.

With Leonard at the Lotus Tree that Friday
night, that photograph of an oversized smiling
Phalanx reminded me of his nickname and that
haircut and his persona, of the origin of it. His
mug just sat up there grandiosely on top the bar,
for this celebration, this wake and pub crawl that
would turn into a party of the derelict kind. People
were everywhere, jammed into dark and wooden
clefts; many old friends, along with some fans who
were wearing orange Malanx jerseys. The place
was electric, crowded and sad and drunk on a
memory that didn't quite add up with my smaller,
more personal memories of my close friend. I
needed a rain forest or a desert maybe, at least an
open space.

Needing air and leaving Leonard to make his
rounds of liquor and conversation, I noticed Mike,
a guy I knew from growing up, who was tending
bar. The place, a touchstone Montrose dive bar, had
what any good culture vulture might expect: red
walls, dim chiaroscuro lighting, velvet paintings
of naked women on the walls, sporadic neon, some
pinball machines, and an extensive selection of
whiskey and bourbon on a tall shelf behind the
bar; chain-smoking creative-looking types on a
back patio with old metal chairs, an eight-foot tall
Mr. Kool-Aid Man in the corner. A four-foot female

Cabbage Patch Kid chained to the aluminum fence, leaning against the Kool-Aid as if she had been overserved. Bottles of Lone Star beer everywhere, combining for a cluttered yet cozy feel of bric-a-brac and kitschy coolness in the crowded, sweaty air of the establishment.

The *Creature from the Black Lagoon* pinball machine rang out as I zeroed in on Mike, noticed his black horn-rimmed glasses and own curious tattoos. I believe I saw an eagle. He grinned white castles at me.

"Holy shit, Bjorn Leonard! How the fuck have you been, man? . . . *Where* have you been?"

"Vermont recently, but been wandering around a while. Pouring drinks myself."

He smiled. "Yep, the grind of the bar." Mike was a kind man, a good kid as I had known him, albeit a bit vain — the kind of kid who put hairspray in his hair several times a day in the bathroom of the high school. Even so, he seemed genuinely to take joy in people. "I guess you are here for Marius's funeral, huh? Really sad, man . . . really sad."

"Yeah, I still don't understand how he died."

"OD'd, man." We clinked glasses and took shots of bourbon. "Rough stuff."

"That just doesn't seem possible." He looked at me, smiled again, poured two more shots.

"Bjorn Leonard? Look at you. That's a hell of a red beard you have." I touched my face, several months' worth.

"I live in the mountains."

"You fit right in in this bar though. Mountain men in the urban jungle."

"Hey, Mike, you have any cocaine? I feel terrible."

He looked at me, gave me an okay sign with his thumb and forefinger, slid me a can of Rodeo Clown made by a local beer company.

In the bathroom, Mike keyed out a few bumps. The bathroom was disgusting, intentionally unkempt with dirty water on the floor, the only available toilet paper sponging the floor's cesspools, but safe enough we were the only ones locked in.

"Are you still acting?" I asked him.

"Quit that a few years ago. Was out in L.A. for a couple years, but that business is filled with sharks. The last embarrassment came when I auditioned for this role. One of those films where a well-known actor plays a main character with Down syndrome. I auditioned for the part of one of his friends and lost out to a guy who actually has Down syndrome."

He kept touching the bridge of his nose as he explained this. "Shit," I said.

"That was the last straw, man. No more acting."

I looked in the small scuffed bathroom mirror at myself, noticing the fatigue in my face, felt sad about it. Mike must have interpreted my weariness, as he gave me a sympathetic look along with his key again.

"But I can't say Houston is any better, even at this bar . . . practically everybody's from the suburbs . . . or Mexican now." Jesus.

"Pretty racist, Mike."

"That's not what I meant. What should I say?"

"Not that."

"Never mind." He keyed another bump. "The thing about Marius's death, man," he said after wiping his face, "is that they ruled it a suicide. Something just doesn't seem right about that to me."

"Suicide?" My stomach dropped a slot, and I keyed another. "He wasn't the type to off himself."

"I know. Marius? He liked a good time, yeah. But for him to kill himself on purpose? I don't buy it." I snorted additional bumps of powder, felt a gash of energy. This would at least help me drink more and propel me through the more awkward vagaries of the night.

Outside the bathroom in the main area of the bar, I located Leonard talking to some folks in the corner at a wooden table. He was pontificating with those oversized clown hands. Leonard isn't exactly a tall man, but his features are bigger than they should be for his height. Big noggin and belly; big hands and feet.

Two huge grounded box fans combined with the Rolling Stones on the vintage jukebox for a rumbling background. Leonard sat underneath a sign that said *Not Texas*, a short beer list of ale not created in the Republic. The pinballs clattered and the machines wailed. A sex doll eyed me from above the entrance of the bathroom doorway where she was nailed.

Leonard: "And, there I was asleep in my underwear, and who was jabbing me hard in the neck but the prodigal son himself!" He snorted, pointed to me as I walked up, and the small crowd gathered around him started laughing. "And, here he is now!"

I hated having to yell to talk. "Hello! Hi, Jackie. Hi, Don. Hello!" These were some people I once knew, friends of The Phalanx too. They gave me hugs, handshakes. "How's it going?"

"I was just telling them about your return, like a queer phoenix in the afternoon!"

"I see."

"What's the story with your tattoos?" asked Jackie. She meant the tattoos on my forearms. I'd had them for years, but to these people these old marks were new and perhaps even ridiculous.

"Just some mistakes of a misspent youth."

"You look like a convict," said Leonard.

"Maybe if it were 1955. Look around, old man. It's normal."

"Pretty squirrelly," he said.

Some fans with Malanx jerseys came over, looking distraught as if they had been crying all day, tattered-looking and puffy around the eyes for the death of what felt to them like a close relative.

"I just can't believe he died," one said, a younger woman. "It's not fair."

"And to die the way he did," another one said. "He was so young . . . and good-looking." This irritated me. These people did not know him — just him as an idea. An attractive image on a screen; a name in capital letters on the back of an expensive jersey. They were crying more and were more outwardly forlorn than those of us who knew him, which didn't seem right. How can you cry for a stranger?

Maybe I had it wrong. Maybe they saw him more purely than I did, in the way that he needed to be seen. I idolized him too but in my own more quiet way. Which felt realistic. But maybe not.

Nothing felt real about any of this. These were associations of strangeness, floating people and objects of my past, a bar and a realm that felt liminal, in between something more practical and logical, tangible even. I knew I wanted to honor The Phalanx, but I also did not know exactly what I was doing there. This wasn't a dream. Dreams, at least the good ones, the lucid ones, can feel life-like and full of possibility in the moment.

In truth, this felt more like the machine-supported coma of a man whose brain had already died.

Confusing as shit . . . all of it. Nonetheless the odd, not-dead body of night continued to rush by in washed commotion — the moving frenzy of fans and friendships. New. Old. I kept going into the bathroom to satisfy my nasal cavity and need for an antidote to anti-sociality. Strangers bought me shots, Mike kept pouring me drinks. I noticed

Leonard getting drunker and louder, and I read the writing on the red walls of the place.

Sudden friends in wake and people whom I had never met were dancing, in huddles of camaraderie, latching onto each other and jumping up with the music while still crying. People hugged me. Drunk people in mourning after midnight, like slipstreamers at a rave on synthetic pills, touched each other in order to feel alive and less alone, in a reconfiguration and reconfirmation of physical presence needed every ten seconds. Some girl I had never met now embracing me, telling me: "It is okay. There, there. You are going to be alright." I didn't know who this person was so close to me. I didn't think I had given off the impression I needed consoling. I was drunk, sure, probably sad-looking, but I wasn't crying. Crying in public is foreign to me, though I could see her bra coming out of her tank top, could feel it — that and her breasts. Her strange smell of lavendar and spoiled milk.

"I will be okay," I said. "What's happening is messed up. And you smell like an alien."

She looked at me as if I were a crippled boy. "There, there. Just let it go." I had to break wind, but I held it in, unlatched myself from this motherly figure, walked in Leonard's direction, and then I did let it go, more gas than fluid.

No one heard this libertine noise amid the blurring and music and overstated exclamations. "Life can be a shit, I know! A goddamned thresher! Cancer of the ass is what got her, the poor thing!" An unguarded young woman in a spring dress Leonard had penned in the corner of the Lotus looked terrified. She made eye contact with me, begging for any person or distraction to save her.

"Hey, Leonard, what's the plan?"

"My plan?! My plan is to get inebriated then

obliterated, make a spectacle of myself! But I will not get arrested! That is my one rule: *Do not get arrested!*"

"Maybe we should go home then." The young woman quietly pretended as if she knew someone on the opposite side of the bar, walked away.

"My son." Leonard held me roughly by the shoulders. "My strong son." He grabbed harder and looked at my face. "My six-foot son."

"6'1."

"Take a drink with me!" I set my hands on the bar. "Mr. Mike the bartender! Two of your finest well bourbons please, sir . . . say, weren't you in a movie or somethin'?"

"A few," Mike corrected.

"Gay porn or straight porn?" Leonard laughed.

Mike eyed me with amusement, the kind mixed with pity for another man's needlessly hassled immediate future.

"Hey, Bjorn," said Jackie, walking up to me. "A lot of us are going to the next bar, the Hi-Lo. You coming?"

"Uh, why not . . . sure thing, Jackie."

"You coming, Mr. Leonard?"

"My dear!" He'd been yelling in that jarring baritone of his. "On a pub crawl a man must do just that! He must crawl. And, since I am not on all fours yet, I will not be scurrying to the next bar. But, my son, my strong son, with those piss poor tattoos and that girly beard, you should accompany this fine woman! Even if she looks somewhat manly."

"Thanks for the permission."

"You always need my permission, boy, whether you know it or not."

We left.

I learned later Leonard had gotten himself kicked out of the Lotus Tree. He got too drunk, his overt friendliness towards strangers interpreted as belligerence. Mike had to calm him down after Leonard said he was going to punch him in the teeth.

Outside the bar, Mike said he couldn't get him to leave until he had threatened to call the police. Leonard, remembering his one rule, stumbled home.

He didn't crawl.

#4

Here in a non-tourist, non-ski Colorado mountain town one or two lives away from urban Texas bars, I think about this:

That need to find a formula. To connect the fractals of street signs and family and a young man's life.

I don't drink to get drunk now.

I occasionally eat a modest amount of legal marijuana; I go to bed early, wake up, put on boots and warm clothes and walk around nameless trees, descending a mountain, removed from cities, and I pour drinks for maybe 30 quiet people every day.

Think about this though: ancient Athens had 250,000 people.

And in 1800, the largest American city had 60,000.

Contemporary Houston has over 2 million, those beautiful ants pulverizing each other on the highway.

This mountain town has 278 citizens.

I still don't have a phone, nor do I look at screens, and as I now more slowly consume — as I eat and walk more casually, I remember those days as a drunken, blurry obstacle course with no finish line. I remember not knowing what I was doing.

Anyway, as Leonard would say, "even snow picks up shit in a storm."

Let's get back to that shit.

#5

We walked two blocks east on Westheimer to the Hi-Lo, the place gathering a charge with the liquids-enhanced entourage of The Phalanx in wake.

The bar was two levels, cave dark with few lamps. Shape-shifting crowds around the bar and on the front porch area building a Friday night dynamism with the shady-looking patrons of the neighborhood.

A punk-sounding, maybe garage rock noise of a band came from upstairs.

The culminated kick of cocaine had made me more sociable, and I now spoke with different people, making for quick conversations imbued with others' short attention spans, the drinks coming even faster too, as I approached the kind of drunkenness wherein one has a tenuous command of the senses. Jackie, a pleasant girl I had known since middle school, now a hairdresser in the neighborhood, was looking after me in her way. I felt I could talk to her.

"All these people for Marius, many who did not really know him, pisses me off."

"I understand what you mean," she said. "It feels less personal with people other than those who grew up with him, friends that have known him for so long."

"He was a likeable guy. A great person. I understand how he connected with people, even as an athlete, but I miss my friend, you know? I miss my friend. I want to talk to him, and all of this bullshit at these bars is not helping. This shit is fake!"

"When was the last time you saw him, Bjorn?"

"He came out to Vermont." I laughed. "That damn *Triumph*. A couple months ago."

I was living in staff housing adjacent to a tennis and ski resort in Stowe, Vermont. A nice view of the mountains. Good air out there, especially for the Northeast, a respectable place for quiet, which clashed with The Phalanx's damn motorcycle he came in on. He roared up sans helmet on a vintage gray 1952 Triumph 6T motorcycle not designed for cross-country riding. It shook and sputtered his entire trip, but it looked smooth enough he thought.

"What are you doing?"

He laughed, massaged his forearms. "Man, I *am sore*."

"That thing looks horrible for a long trip."

"This was the same motorcycle my father rode as a young man."

"I see," I said.

"It's been a good work-out. I felt bad for the guy who sold it to me. He was going through a tough time."

"I can imagine . . . I'm sure you gave him too much money for it too."

"Doesn't matter."

On my days off we took hikes in the medium-sized grey mountains, went swimming in a river, lay on large rocks for the sun. Shared drinks with wives who had parlayed their days with tennis on the resort's outdoor clay courts and lounging on massage tables and around the spa's pools. This was a world The Phalanx and I were unfamiliar with, a fantasy and pause from our usual more urban and less glamourous conditions, though he had encountered a bit more of the good life recently due to professional soccer. I spoke with him about his future aims. He knew his soccer career had a fairly short shelf life, and he talked about moving back to Denver maybe the mountains after his first career had ceased, perhaps to open a small business with the cash we always talked about saving; we brainstormed ideas for the types of bar or restaurant we could own and run together.

But mainly we fantasized about living in the same place again and doing things like drinking beer and playing pool and not being bothered by bullshit. These are the more simple moments I remember. Conversations we had away from cities, on porches smoking and bearing ourselves. On occasion I would make a soccer game in one of the places his team was playing in, meet up with him after, get a few drinks and reconnect, but those moments blend together. I don't remember them as well as these other quieter times, wherein we were just two friends with a mutual understanding. He was a great soul, the most giving person I've ever known, and it wasn't unusual for him to give a hundred dollar bill to a stranger or pick up the bar tab for someone he had just met. He didn't care about money the way most people do.

Even when he was about to leave Vermont he tried to give me a check for a thousand dollars.

"No way," I said. "I don't want your money. Save it for when we start a business together. Besides, a professional soccer player who rides the bench in this country doesn't make more than a plumber. What do you make like 60K a year? You might be better off bartending."

He laughed his great laugh. "I know you could use it. I know you're not getting enough hours."

"No way."

But it didn't matter. I found over two hundred dollars, probably all the cash he had in his wallet at the time, placed next to the lamp on my nightstand when I returned to my room that night. "It all circulates," he had said.

He was this. He gave all of himself — his time, his money, his energy . . . in the end.

"You know who is here, right?" Jackie mentioned, bringing us back to the Hi-Lo. "Merle."

"Merle? Really . . . where?"

"Just listen." I looked upward to the next level past the balcony, saw a person singing. Well, yelling. An angry woman screaming into a microphone, her primal sounds for the crowd of responsive onlookers.

> *Get your suds*
> *Get your suds*
> *at the quickie mart!*
>
> *Get your cigs*
> *Get your cigs*
> *at the quickie mart!*
>
> *Get your cocks*
> *Get your cocks*
> *at the quickie mart!*
>
> *Get your cunts*
> *Get your cunts*
>
> *at . . . the . . . QUICKIE MART!*

There were roars and fuck yeah's . . . *Fuuuuuuuck yeah!* . . . a bang . . . and a bam and some other shit.

"That's her?" I couldn't believe this was the same Merle, the only serious girlfriend of my Houston days. The one who had caused me the most significant amount of pain before I had become basically detached in relationships. She wasn't my first, but she was the first one to show me something.

She looked different here from my memories. No longer a girl, older now with dyed hair an unrealistic red, nearly purple, pinned back away from her face. Huge blue eyes and pale skin of an androgynous visage, yet the resemblance of the unique nearly haunted face I had always been drawn to. I walked upstairs into the crowd.

She was wailing in a black dress, black combat boots, white bandanas tied around her wrists. A big hoop earring in one ear with small wooden multi-colored birds perched around the other earring with a fluorescent feather pointing downward. She had tattoos nearly everywhere on her exposed light skin, and I remembered when she had received her first one, the large sacred heart on the upper part of her chest below her neck. She had gripped my hand hard the whole way through. I could see the top of it now, its flames and spirals of vines entangled around a bulging heart.

She grasped the microphone here as if she wanted to kill it, pumped her free fist with the sound of the drums — the crowd yelled with her, many arms uplifted.

No, this was not the same girl I had known. That girl was aloof yet sweet, sometimes halfway gone and eccentric and creative in how she spoke and gestured, used to making frequent unsure pauses. This woman in front of me was forceful, a presence that lacked uncertain terms. The loud guitar sounds were rivaled by her commanding voice. "*Take me home! Take me home!*" she yelled strongly though nearly indecipherably as the crowd yelled with her: "*Mother . . . fucker . . . TAKE ME HOME!*"

Merle's band was called Two Birds One Stone — a three-piece act with a female guitarist and female lead vocalist, a male drummer, that had some clout in some of the smaller inner Houston loop venues, and Merle especially I came to find out was infamously revered in select scenester spheres. The band finished up its last song, getting louder and louder with every encouragement, the shirtless drummer pounding away, the guitarist with her three scarves thrashing about, until its lead singer was sweating and seemingly wiped out from her vocal and physical exertion. She was home.

Some form of home I guess.

Finding me after the set on the front patio, she took a cigarette from the pack in my front shirt pocket, put a hand on her head. "Bjorn. Thought you died, man."

"Only wandering the earth."

"Always the histrionic one."

"*Histrionic.* That's a hell of a word."

"Don't act dumb. You always had a surprisingly big vocabulary."

"I have my verbiage moments."

"Ha."

"Not bad I guess for a person with just his G.E.D. *Irregardless*, you're the one who yells on stage now."

She gave out another quick monosyllabic laugh. "Ha ... it's fun." She smoked her cigarette with a poised control I did not remember. "This music has been a good time."

"Seems people like it."

"Yeah. Word. It's a rush. *Sensory.*" She pronounced this last word slowly.

"So what else have you been doing with yourself? Other than yelling for the cool kids?"

"Waitressing, bartending. Doing some painting." She paused, looked at the crowd on the patio. "Bought a duplex with this guy."

"Let me guess. He's fifty years old and he runs an art gallery somewhere around here. Used to be your mentor." She half laughed, ground out her cigarette with a military boot.

"Close. He's in his forties and a film professor."

"I knew it."
"Did you?"

Aside from Leonard and an unstable household, I also left Houston because I was told Merle had slept with a guy who worked at a gas station near the high school where she bought her cigarettes and weed. A dick-fuck in his late twenties who seemed to have a thing for high school girls. Merle was just another notch on this guy's bedpost, I knew she never cared about this asshole, but as a teenager the possibility of an older man had intrigued her. Being just a teenager myself I couldn't compete with the maturity of these other men out of school, and after hearing she had slept with him, it made it that much easier for me to leave. Merle apologized, but it was another reminder of my center not holding. Nearly everyone I cared about had betrayed me one way or another, which in turn made me care about even less moving forward — a subsequent immediate world not typically of investment. In effect: only went and did what I wanted while skirting around the periphery, never getting too attached nor involved. To perform the opposite would have lent that part of myself I had no comfortable desire in practically carrying forth.

She looked at me, scratched the top of her sacred heart. "What are you doing now? Want to go to a party?"

"I am supposed to be on this pub crawl wake for Marius." I looked into the throng of people, a sea of smoke and swallows. "But that's breaking up now it looks like. People are mainly just drunk and at the bar like any other night. I don't see much mourning going on now, actually."

"I heard about that. I'm sorry, Bjorn. I know how

much he meant to you." I thought she had no idea. The Phalanx had been the only reliable element of Houston for me. The only person and real friend who had been endearingly consistent. I could depend on him, yet now he was gone — and this ex-girlfriend I barely recognized was in front of me.

"Thanks . . . so I guess you never saw him around."

"Here and there. But he knew a lot of people. *Lots* of different people. It was always hard to pin him down for anything more than a cigarette. Never the type of guy to stand still anyway, almost literally. I can't remember the last time I saw that dude sitting down."

"So where's the party?"

"Pretty close."

If was almost three in the morning, and the party wasn't that close. We had to take Merle's green 1978 Pontiac Parisienne downtown from Montrose to get there. After parking that boat of a car, we walked up to Neal's Clothing Company, which was not a clothing company at all but a bar in the process of being remodeled. Next to Neal's was a bar that had just closed for the night. I stood on the old cobblestone sidewalk, the steel tracks for the light rail behind me on Main Street. Ground-out cigarette butts scattered the stone. A display window of the closed bar showcased headless torsos of gold and silver mannequins fully exposed — one with lingerie made of rope. There were shade-less lampstands, Native American headdresses, and antique vases. A black lone star, above these items, did not shine. These places were just two of the many bars and clubs in renovated early-to-mid twentieth-century Houston buildings, reminiscences of a booming past that would soon match a booming current. We bypassed the front door of Neal's and the closed bar next to it. I noticed the broken legs of a mannequin turned upside down. At the foot of another door next to the entry doors of the closed bar was an empty PBR can and an empty package of Marlboro Golds. Right outside the door was an ATM machine that looked like it had been scorched to the ground. With graffiti letters scrawled over it, it looked like a sci-fi relic, a non-functioning reminder of a previous era's technology. We walked past all this through the other door up some stairs to a large loft space.

I remember these details in my sleep.

The place first appeared like the back prop room of a playhouse — more mannequins of various shapes donned in outrageous retro outfits. Some fur coats and bell bottoms, boas and plastic costume jewelry of the gaudy kind, enlarged stuffed animals on the floors, old dirty Oriental rugs, and medieval armor of knights — the massive head of a taxidermy moose lay against one wall. A few naked people sat crosslegged in baby pools. A couple hundred more people dressed in various costumes danced slowly to a DJ's beats from a turntable. I sat down in an old orange and black antique chair, my ass on the tiger stripes, by a window that overlooked the downtown Main Street and the blur of myriad bodies trickling out of closing bars to go home or come to places like this one. The Houston nightlife had come a long way.

"I will be right back," Merle said. "I want to say hi to some people I see." I took in the space again. It did feel like a carnival with those baby pools and underwater dancing and headless synthetic beings of fabulousness. I noticed some blown-up photographs of naked celebrities on the walls. That kid from Harry Potter, fully frontal looking confident — naked John Lennon and Yoko Ono seemed assured of themselves, too. Houston was not New York or even Seattle, but it momentarily was considering itself as the center of the universe.

A woman tapped me on the shoulder. "Are you Dale?"

"Who is Dale?"

"I just thought you might be Dale since you're not wearing a disguise. Dale's going to be my life coach. I met him online. Supposed to meet him here."

"Since when does a person meet her life coach on the internet or even at a place like this?"

"I just had a feeling about him," she said, weirdly assured. This woman had on a long gothic dress, narrow straps at the top, a white daisy behind her ear, hair down nearly to her waist. She wore dark sunglasses, and I didn't imagine she could see very well.

"What did you expect to discuss with Dale?"

"He is supposed to help me project my energies in more productive fashions. Something related to transcendental meditation."

I brought out some cocaine from my pocket, lifted a key to my nostril.

"Want some of this for your productive fashions?" She did, inhaled a bump. "So, tell me. Who lives in this place?"

"It belongs to a burlesque dancer." She motioned to a larger woman standing next to the DJ.

"She doesn't look like a dancer."

"I think she just manages some dance troops now." Merle came over to us looking excited.

"Hillary, hi! You've met Bjorn." She gave this woman a hug. "Hillary and I work together at the Emerald," she explained. I nodded as if I knew the Emerald.

"By the way, Bjorn. You should come by tomorrow. I want you to meet someone there."

For a spell I danced with Merle and Hillary.

Merle danced up close to me, took my hand, twirled herself. Even closer, she said into my neck: "Relax, man."

"Sure."

Hillary on my backside was doing some kind of gyrating half-hump, God knows. I mainly ran in place, not into it, as they continued around me. The electronic sounds set forth by the DJ were uncomplicated and repetitive. Some guy was giving another guy a blowjob in one of the baby pools. The mannequins increasingly became naked as the afterpartygoers stripped the fur coats and boas and accompaniments for their evocative though leisurely performative acts. That moose head remained untouched — and I drank more alcohol, attempted to lose myself, but it wasn't working. Not the cocaine now, none of it. I needed to get on with it, walk away from the processed syrup of the city, a long exhausted way from what many consider a good time. "Hey, y'all want to go upstairs to the orgie room?" Hillary asked. I looked at Hillary in her sunglasses and Merle in her boots. An image flickered, but I decided against it.

"Nah, not this time," I said.

"Merle?"

Merle shook her head. "Just going to take this asshole home."

"Maybe you'll find your life coach up there," I said.

Merle drove cautiously in the green Parisienne, and we didn't say much until we were parked in front of Leonard's place. "I think you need sleep You look really far gone, man."

"It's been a bad couple of days."

"Well . . . come and see me tomorrow."

I said I would and removed myself from her car. From the outside, I could see all of the lights were still on in Leonard's place. I looked back at Merle before closing the door.

"Thanks for the ride."

"Word," she said.

"You look good, Merle." She smiled. Those wooden birds shook as she winked a lone eye.

"And you look like garbage . . . but you'll be all right. Just get some sleep, dude."

I looked back at the lit duplex. "We'll see if that's possible."

"Go easy on the guy. He always meant well."

I could hear loud howling. "You have no idea."

Leonard stood in the middle of his living room, yelling and projecting his big frame up to the ceiling. "*Hoooweeeee! Life is a shit river! A shiiiiiiit rivaaaaaaaaaar! Hooweeee . . . hoowee!*"

His voice was a scary kind of loud, deep within a well of lost hope and a return to old fears that felt newfound. Willie Nelson played on full volume, but Leonard yelled louder than that, standing there in his underwear, his red face sweating nonstop. I turned the music down. Chicken bones were strewn about the carpet. Seems he had taken apart and gnarled one of those grocery store-cooked rotisserie chickens, devoured it messily with zero utensils in his drunkenness.

"Time to go to bed," I said.

"I will not. *Noooo-ottttt! Hoooweeee!* The girl has the bitch, boy! The girl has the bitch! And where is the dog?!" He raised his arms into the air.

"*The dog*. What the fuck are you talking about?" He raised his arms even higher, yelled out his lungs with full hysterical expenditure.

"She says things! Enticements. But the bitch means harm, boy. She means harm! The dog, the shit dog comes down to rip your throat out! Rip it out . . . in this . . . fucking . . . *shit river!*

Hoowaaa! Hoooooooweeeee!"

He picked up an end table and threw it against the wall, took off his white undershirt to expose his fleshy mass, rubbed his huge stomach.

"Why have you come home, boy?! You fucking ... *shit!*" He pronounced this last word with a loud but slow relished drawl. He stepped towards me with his hands raised while I stood there, quickly remembering the many moments between us. I was ready to pop the old man in the face if need be.

"You know why."

"For ... your ... friend. The little soccer player? A junkie. A fucking junkie who offed himself! *Sheeee-it. Hoowaaaa!*"

"He was a much better man than you."

"Honey." He was looking about for someone who was not there now. "Honey!" He looked at me. "I cannot *control* the shit floating in the *rivaaah*! You're just a child. Your mother left. The *bitch* left!"

I pushed him barely and he easily fell into the couch, showing a quick grin like some game had been played. "Drink some water, go to bed. And pick up these fucking chicken bones!"

He smiled that red face again. "Honey? *Hoowaaa* ... the prodigal don't mean shit." I didn't have time for this routine. I was tired and drunk myself, and had seen this demented act countless times.

I decided to sleep in the bathtub. I ran the water and locked the door, sat down in the tub and put a wet wash rag over my face — yet I could still hear the ceaseless wails and rumblings. He played his country music louder, stomped around for a time, before I finally heard him snoring.

I did not know what was possessing him, only had a vague repetitive notion of his earlier traumas and adult difficulties.

I also knew he was a bad drunk.

But I felt for him somewhat — yet finally realized he was just a restless child who would lash out whenever life got messy.

Life is unfair, sure. Life is unfair. That's right. But we can either choose to destroy the world we live in, or we can choose to sleep, pretend all we need is a thin barrier of rag on our faces, maybe some warm water.

Or maybe there's a third option.

If you let it, madness can fade into the past, eventually start snoring on the couch — only a small photograph of a horrific time. You need only take it, that temporary photograph, out of your backpocket to look at on occasion. If you then want to know how relieving it is to forget.

A person can move on.

It took me a while to realize all of this. And Leonard should hear this too.

We do not choose our fathers.

(Drugs don't ask questions,
so how are you going to say 'no'? — *Ed.)*

SATURDAY

"Life ain't about making apologies. It's about making up some lost time with some action. So, you're welcome."

—Boyd Leonard, *sober.*

#6

This story is measurably about names. Names and labels and headlines — but especially about names.

Leonard named me after Bjorn Borg, the Scandinavian Golden Child. The Ice Borg, the tennis great.

When I was born in the hospital in Houston in '89, several names circulated his head.

One look at me, with John McEnroe playing on the TV in the hospital in the background, and he remembered the icon. Leonard was not a tennis player, had never touched a racquet, nor have I for that matter, but as he explained it he had heard a story by the announcer on the TV in the hospital that day about Borg losing in the 1981 U.S. Open finals to John McEnroe. After the match Borg skipped the awards ceremony and got into his Mercedes, defiantly and feverishly ending his professional career in the peak of his powers at the age of 26. Leonard liked this story, and he liked the name, and in his perverse mind my namesake was not in honor of Borg's former glory but was a reminder to Leonard of his sudden disappearing own youth and glory days with the emergence of having a baby; with the acute loss of freedom, even though he was already 34. The good times officially over in his mind, Patsy gave birth in the spirit of Borg shutting himself off in his car.

And Leonard never wanted a kid.

He reminded me of this last bit several times along with the story of my namesake (his version of it, at least) while he was drunk. He thought he was helping, but actually he was just reminding me that I had been stamped with the moniker of a burned-out star, with associations of regret and hypotheticals of what could have been.

Which reminds me . . .

The Phalanx garnered his name by more honorable means. Marius Malanx as a young boy was spastic, would not stop talking and goofing around long enough to listen to the coach. And even though we all knew Marius was an athletic freak, the coach did not put him in the first couple games. Finally when Marius got on the field in the second half of a game, he received the ball up top and maneuvered his way quickly through the defense. He did this a few times, scoring a handful of goals in little time. After the game the coach called Marius over: "Malanx," he said. "You are a spaz, but you play the game like a damn phalanx."

The name stuck. He always seemed like more than one person.

As I left Leonard at his house that morning to sleep off his hangover and suspend his atrocities, I took his crap truck to go see Merle at the Emerald, a strip-club joint off the 45 highway going south of the city near the university.

The place hadn't been renovated for decades. Merle behind the bar, Hillary on a stage above doing a hippie-ish dance as if she were outside in the natural air, her long hair and organic breasts exposed for a few gentlemen at her stiletto-clad feet. She was completely shaven, and I wondered if her life coach would approve of this.

Merle spotted me and waved me over, slid me some bourbon with water. The place was windowless — dirty and uninspired, but Merle looked beautiful enough behind the bar. Those tattoos. "I can't believe you of all people work in a strip club," I said.

"The place is pretty low-key." I looked around. For a strip club the space was well lit. No one seemed to care if you could see stretch marks or your face in reflection.

Felt more like a dive bar.

"Why is this place open so early anyway?"

"We do a lot of business in the morning and during the day. A lot of these old guys get off late shifts and come here before going home. They like the buffet. We actually don't do as well at night." I noticed a table of steak and eggs and other breakfast food in the corner.

"A lap dance with breakfast? This is the least glamorous strip-club I have ever been in," I said.

"I know . . . it's a job. A few of these old guys do tip really well."

"You ever get up on stage?"

"No way, man. I only dance for dudes I'm with." And I remembered.

"Does your professor approve of these work conditions?"

"He rationalizes it, thinks it's salt of the earth. Unpretentious in its insinuations."

"It insinuates taking off your clothes for money."

She dismissed this, poured herself some vodka. "At least I can drink on the job . . . and my band plays here sometimes." She took a sip. "Come with me. We don't need to get into a discussion about feminist morals. There's someone I want you to meet."

We pushed past the old men and their morning release, the naked girls, Hillary. Hair metal played out of speakers. This titty bar felt forgotten, with its shabby lounge chairs and tarnished stripper poles — small clear plastic cups that contained overly priced well alcohol, all-you-can-eat brunch for $12.99.

In the back dressing room some women were sitting down cramped in front of mirrors, applying make-up and adjusting themselves. I sensed meth molecules in the air — a beauty pageant gone belly up on the barely started day.

Merle motioned to one woman in front of a mirror with a light blue nightgown. She was too skinny, almost pretty, having caked the make-up on.

"Bjorn, this is Lizzie. Lizzie knew Marius fairly well."

This woman turned away from her reflection, offered her bony hand. "Nice to meet you." I could barely understand what she was saying — a low slurred cadence.

"Lizzie, tell him what you told me."

She turned back to the mirror, started putting on eyeliner. "Marius told me about you."

"He was a good friend."

"I am sorry." God, that slur. She looked at herself again in the mirror. "Well, something happened to him. Was partying with him the night he died — drinking and everything but nothin' too crazy." She set down her eyeliner, looked at me through the mirror's reflection. I had no idea how old she was. "I left him at his place and he just said he was tired, had to wake the next day for a work-out or somethin', but he was nervous acting. Somethin' he was worried about rubs me wrong, doesn't add up to him dying like he did."

"What's that?"

"He kept saying that some guys were coming for him, threatening him, like that."

"What kind of guys?"

"Somethin' about the Greeks . . . at the Parthenon. That place in Montrose? He asked me to stay with him that night, but I had to meet up with this guy. It's just the way he was talking. He seemed so worried. Real tired but worried."

"Worried about what?"

"That maybe something bad was going to happen. Like these guys were going to do something to him."

"But why would these Greeks want to do something bad to him?"

"I don't know. Not any good explanation anyway. I just have a feeling that somethin' happened that we don't know about . . . at least not in the way they say."

I looked in the mirror at her. Even with the make-up she seemed like a woman with few delusions. "It's such a shame," she said. "Marius was always so good to me. I have a little one at home . . . a six-year-old. I would tell him not to, but I always found money in my purse from him. He always told me to spend it on my daughter." She looked at me now away from the mirror, her eyes and surrounding area older than the rest of her face. "He was such a sweetheart."

All true. The Phalanx was always giving time and money to people — people who needed it. Homeless people and the wayward and broke, but it wasn't just the money. He wasn't a philanthropist in the sense that some other professional athletes are. He didn't volunteer at charities or visit children's hospitals on holidays. He talked to people, helped them — listened to them, then gave them whatever they needed: cash, some conversation, drugs, a place to sleep. I don't think there was much ego in it.

He believed in good intentions of others, a kindness to it all. I never remembered him not carrying this forth. He could get frustrated, sure, mainly at some dickhead's mistreatment of another person — but he also believed down deep he could transcend the nature of a bully.

Maybe this was a vice.
Maybe not.

Back at the bar I sipped on my drink, looked across at Merle.

"What the fuck, Merle?" I said this with little emphasis. "Why did you have me come all the way down here just to get this cryptic, evasive story? You could have told me this last night."

"I guess, but I wanted you to hear it for yourself . . . and . . . I wanted to see you again."

"*See* me again? We could have met somewhere else."

"Man, I had to work. Don't act like an asshole. I didn't want to tell you last night because I didn't think you could handle it . . . you looked like you were going out of your head. At one point I looked over while you were dancing, and you looked like you were going to fall over. Thought it'd be better to tell you in person after you had gotten some sleep. I wanted you to know that something isn't right. You said last night that Marius was not the type to kill himself." Jesus.

"What am I supposed to do?"

"I don't know. Ask around."

"*Ask around?*"

"If you don't think he killed himself then you should find out what was going on with the guy."

"Sure . . . why not." I looked around that bar and made a sweeping gesture with my arm to indicate the secondhand spirit of the larger place — the one beyond the bounds of this small and naked window-free warp. "Houston is such a shithole."

"Home is where you shit, man."

"I guess I don't want a bathroom in my house."

She gave me her middle finger; I showed her my middle finger in return, and we finished our drinks.

But mind you I had regained that every-other-hour impulse. The feeling to leave the city, forget about all of it again, but I also figured what the shit. I might as well play detective for a day, see if I could answer some questions. Marius was not a junkie.

As I left I saw Hillary dancing to a hair metal song. Her long legs wrapped around the pole. I could see her ribs, and I imagined she had some guy she could go see.

As did I.

#7

I don't need photographs of the past.

They live in my brain, and I can't drop them. My family lives in me — the hurts of my father and great and great great grandparents, my mother, my mother's parents and their parents, their hurts reside in my brain and nervous system — compartments of consciousness, rooms I walk into and visit, (re)visit, connect with the losses, heart ache(s), the hurts of fathers and mothers and children, and the lives we have shared all of our lives.

I fought with my father, yes, there's that history, and my mother left; I dropped out of high school with no aspirations for college — in another life maybe things would have gone differently, but in this one I figured I could get by . . . started reading paperbacks and teaching myself — have been a dishwasher, bartender, waiter, some other jobs. Friends in Austin and Houston. Marius, some other people, some other friends I picked up here and there, but mainly drifted around.

Few things, less clunky, never had much cash. I liked the lightness, the ease of getting up, putting everything I own in one bag and leaving — few attachments, better this way, the idea of the exit. Many wanderers tell the same.

I've lived in over twelve towns and cities in less than a decade.

And they say you can't run from your problems, but I disagree. At least two prongs of a fork tell

you as much: You can leave behind the details you
won't miss, and there is the hope that memory
will haze into the ether: Those details of the
bigoted manager of the restaurant you worked
at in Oklahoma. The woman you slept with in
Austin while her three-year-old daughter Anais
was asleep in the next room. The ex-husband
that wanted to murder you. The drugdealer in
Brooklyn named Spank who pulled a gun on you
for strange reasons — the graduate student in
Providence who cheated on you and lied about it,
the drunk tank in Worcester where a man named
George Jackson said the devil was inside of him.

You move on — from throwing up and passing out
on the bathroom floor of a bar in Portland, Maine,
to getting choked out by a bouncer in Lafayette,
Indiana, to howling at the sunrise over rooftops
in Baltimore to hitchhiking in a stranger's stolen
car in Ashville, North Carolina . . . and that time
in Pittsburgh you hit a pimp by the name of Dallas
in his good tooth — you move away because you
want to drop these memories, better and worse,
at the edges of the city limits of these places —like
leaving boxes on the curb, with a feeling of no
longer needing belongings nor memories as you
drive or walk away from town, hoping the next
containers of details will be better — not a
duplication of past variables and materials but
actually better — in the senses of hope and
momentary idealism mixed with an allergy to
repetition.

But you know, in other moments, this is a lie . . .
you come to/wake up . . . you know these are
falsehoods . . . because yes your family lives in you.
You realize this as you drive and walk through
towns and American cities — and around Houston
now through swirling cement . . . the spirals of
construction. For, I've eaten the plates, the plates,
every plate of food in this huge city. I've taken

all this one has to offer. As Leonard said it once, "let me tell you something, Bjorn, life is a damn buffet; sure you've got vegetables and meat on there but you also have shit on there on trays. And sometimes you have to eat the shit. You remember that the next time you have to make a choice, wherever you are going now."

And it's true. I can't begin to tell you what the point of being human is. But I can say I don't kill people, don't rape anyone, don't steal very often and try to keep my lying to a minimum. I strive to be as decent as I know how — and within my powers and constitution I then strive to reduce the amount of harm I cause, but even *then* I'm limited; even then I am bound.

My earliest memory:

From the age of two and a half maybe three, Patsy was running water in the tub, told me to get in. She left the bathroom briefly, and in her absence, due I can only imagine now to anxiety and small-child terror, I exerted a big poop in the tub.

Shocked, I left the bathroom, flailed naked down the hallway and around to the living room where I hid behind a window curtain. I could hear her asking, "Bjorn! Bjorn, are you okay?" I stood behind that curtain with fear and wonder for a long time, felt like, before she found me. "Bjorn? what are you doing behind there?"

My bawling wouldn't stop. I kept crying as she embraced me again and again.

And this is my conscious beginning point — fear, a drastic response, shame, and tears. Seems I've been duplicating this episode, this memory, my entire life.

Sure. As a memory on top of memory — now remembering from afar, from a higher altitude respite with snow all around me outside this small

house in the mountains — I remember thinking
and driving in that crap truck around that city
that weekend, attempting to find some personal
rhythm in the urban entropy. For . . . yes . . .
the Houston highways feel grand though poorly
planned. All wrong. A person feels his anxiety
while driving them at first — the endless lanes and
own unspoken aggressive pact of machination.
Then after a time the stress becomes embodied
and habitual — until the release of these latent
nerves gets expelled with eating ungodly plates
and drinking and running around in a city of
decadence in the sagging heat. I felt this tension as
a person feels the stress of riding on the back of a
large untrained animal in the bardo. My synapses,
those memories too, were hectically firing through
as I drove the traffic in the truck, the labyrinthine
cement not quite a video game. Not exactly the
true world either. And knowing I needed to talk to
some people, I made some calls as I always had —
on the rare pay phone or on the borrowed cellular
phones of strangers — and asked around: called
Mike and spoke to a few other voices, in between
cans of Lone Star and driving.

While in traffic with my thoughts, those
memories — give/take, better/worse than.

What have you, sure.

Sure enough. Past and present bleed and blend.

These are my photographs.

#8

Julie's Donuts sits in a little strip mall off Montrose Boulevard close to Midtown. Clashing with its massive yellow and red marquee that was created during the days of Jimmy Carter, the exterior of the small business is nondescript — but its kolaches have been made by inspired hands, and their donuts beat most.

Inside the place among the stretch of low-rent fixtures — gaudily tiled floor and a faded menu containing prices from a long-gone time taped to the glass of the kolache-donut display case, I noticed a Chinese calendar on the wall, along with framed photographs of the Eiffel Tower and a rain forest; two old grey men in tank tops sat eating donuts and drinking coffee, a teenager with a University of Texas t-shirt ordering to go, behind him a man down on his luck with what looked like someone else's baggy clothes, all there for the tender goodness made by a few generations of hands.

The kid with the UT shirt spoke of a woman who had been there the other day who had showed everyone her boob. "I don't know why she did it. Jordan was here working the counter, and she just pulled it out, flapped it around. All Jordan did was write it up." The teenage kid in sunglasses working the register only shrugged, put the UT shirt's dollar tip in the jar on the countertop.

Towards the back of the place in a hallway next to the bathrooms, a young cop sat at a table looking at his phone and drinking a Mountain Dew.

He wore a mustache, which was a new addition to his beefy mug. He had the gut and compact muscular build of a guy who attended Crossfit and ate cheap steaks after.

"Magnum P.I., how the fuck are you?"

He looked up from his phone, smiled, felt his 'stache. "Just a bet I have with the guys." He gave me an overly firm handshake. "Bjorn Leonard. How's your dad?"

"Still passed out this time of day."

"I always loved that lunatic. He hasn't been arrested lately has he?"

"Who's to say. Can't keep up. Listen Chad, excuse me — *Officer Carr*, what have you found out? They say Marius killed himself . . . but that doesn't make much sense to me."

"No." He considered this. "I guess the way we always knew Marius was that he enjoyed life."

I nodded.

"Listen. I did check on this after you called me. All I know: The officers at his residence found a needle in his arm. The medical investigator's autopsy said lethal dose of heroin, some cocaine . . . alcohol, marijuana."

"They found him with a needle in his arm?"

"Happens unfortunately."

I drifted off into the street, my mind did. The cars were honking in clustered crawl, and the car wash across the boulevard sprayed its business everywhere.

"How's the wife?" Rumor had it Chad Carr was working on his marriage. His wife had stepped out for a time. With a woman — only to come back to repair the domestic suburban dreams of all-but-forgotten Eisenhower-era intentions. Chad believed in institution, in the tightness of it. I only wish I had the stomach for it.

But Carr was all right, for the rigid type. He was the goalie for our high school team, always the guy to get *too* amped before a game — but his militarism forgiven because he was the kind of teammate you could count on to show up and do his best. After all, a soccer goalie, perhaps more than any other position, especially one that was 5'9" on a good day as Chad was, needs to be disciplined, even if ideologically misguided.

"All good on my end. Outside of being a cop, just living the boring life of an adult . . . not to say I don't seek out a little *strange* now and then."

"Yeah? How does your wife feel about that?"

He looked at me as if I were out of my mind. "She wouldn't know of it."

"And what would you do if you found out she was getting a little strange on the side."

"Would kill him . . . and then I would kill her. She should never tell me." I thought about how he had conveniently used the wrong pronoun to refer to his wife's potential exploits. He then folded his paper and creased this thought away. "Naw, Heidi and I are doing fine." Taking out his phone, he showed me some pictures of his two young girls. "You play soccer anymore?"

"Not at all. Stopped that a long time ago. Marius was the only one who had any use for that."

"He *was* doing alright . . . finally got some playing time. He had the most powerful left foot, the beautiful freak. Glad I never had to go against that in an official game."

"A needle in his arm?"

Soapy tainted chemical water dominated the cemented lot of the carwash across the street. Chad turned his head to see what I was looking at. I have this habit of staring off into nothing as if it's something.

I once drove out to Colorado for Thanksgiving. My car broke down in Pueblo. Not the place you would want to vacation. The Phalanx and I were supposed to connect then drive to the mountains, get away for the holiday, but once the car broke down it put into motion a sequence of events that did not include beautiful terrain.

He picked me up though. He had a five-day break from the university and his team. Something about Pueblo terrified me, still does. Maybe it's the down-at-the-heel strip malls in the high desert next to a river that has been bastardized, or the idea that its settlers gave up, thought it was just good enough, before never making it further west to the mountains or north to the larger already established town. Whatever it was doesn't matter now.

The Phalanx arrived on his cycle ready to blow it out. He had bottles of bourbon, beer, some cocaine, and a little baggy of black tar opium.

"Jesus," I said when he showed me all of this. "I only brought some weed. You sure you don't want some needles to inject some of this shit?"

"No way, brother. I hate needles. You know that. Always have."

"I know. You couldn't donate blood if your life depended on it."

"The look of it makes me want to puke then pass out."

"Of all the things to be scared of."

"The fear doesn't make sense," he said, laughing. "We inhale and sniff fine. But injection's a graduation I do not want to attend."

We smoked the opium first because I had never tried it. It made me feel numb pretty quick like a full-bodied massage; then I took some jolts of cocaine — then bourbon, then beer to even out. We were still in the parking lot of a fast food burger place. My car was dead and couldn't get looked at until the next day, which even then was unlikely because of Thanksgiving.

We smoked cigarettes, decided to go to a bar next

door. The idea of riding up to Denver in the cold that night on his rickety motorcycle didn't seem worth it.

The bar was at a pizza place. The pizza was crap, but the drinks were cheap. An older gentleman next to us on a stool decided he liked us. He spoke about living "off the grid," owing money to differing parties, being forced out to drift.

"The debts accumulate. Then people start to hate you. Forget wives and children. They hate you on principle. Everyone else just smells the money-owing scent of you, wants no part."

This old guy, of reported deep Italian heritage — he kept reminding us that he was "Renzo the Third in a Row" — though it was clear he did not have much connection to family, Italian or otherwise.

"Living off the grid seems alright. Maybe some freedom in it?"

"Bingo," said this Renzo. "Less stress out of bounds, but no one knows you long enough to care about you." This guy had a red stocking cap. Hard lines on the face, crow's feet around the eyes, from probably smoking too much.

I was already pretty far gone off substances; The Phalanx asked the man about filial love.

"Oh yeah. But just know this. No place is perfect. No job is perfect, and no woman for hell is perfect." He drank his beer.

"Where does Pueblo fit into all of this?"

"Shoot, Pueblo is a waste. Merely a stop-off. But it's a place where people don't want to come to find me. My ex-wife does not want to find me here I know that."

We all were quiet for a time as we watched a basketball game on the small television above the bar.

This Renzo started up again: "See that point guard there, he's an Asian. You don't see many Asians playing American sports at a high level.

But Bruce Lee, now there was an athlete. The best we have ever seen. Bruce could have done anything. NFL wide receiver, NBA point guard. Short stop for MLB. Can you imagine?"

"I can imagine," The Phalanx said. "The grace of it, he had that magic. The kind that applies to any situation. He had it."

Another old guy at the bar chimed in: "Sure, the trick is to treat your body like water. But I think Bruce was too short, guys."

"He was tall enough," said The Phalanx.

Renzo smiled, raised his glass. "Here's to Bruce's magic, boys . . . and to not knowing what day it is."

"Fuck all," that other old guy slurred.

Renzo stayed by our side, and more old men and birds of paradise came and went out. We interchangeably left the bar to go to my brokedown car or into the bathroom to put more junk into our systems. The substances weren't the point. The implication was that we could handle most anything. "How does a person abuse a substance?" I remember Leonard asking one time. "The substance tries to abuse you . . . if you let it," he said, answering his own question.

Snow covers shit in a storm. But I couldn't handle it. In the parking lot of that pizza place-bar, I smoked some marijuana as a late-night cap and then proceeded to puke my guts — then gagged and gagged. It was the combination of everything. The puke didn't even look real — the colors of the spewage play-time green, but I could see my life in it. The Phalanx was good about it, encouraging. "Get it out, brother. *Gag* out the negative. Make it all new." He knew what to say. "Puke today. Rest tomorrow. You'll be perfect." I don't remember him showing signs of intoxication at all. I remember his decency.

The Phalanx put the drunk Renzo in the

backseat of my car, and the old Italian dodger was snoring before my head could spin again.

"You just going to let him sleep and snore in the car?"

"Why not?" he said. "The guy could use a bed as bad as we do. And it's Thanksgiving tomorrow."

I still felt sick but nothing else seemed to be coming back up. I stepped off to the side of the parking lot away from the light.

Off the grid? There is no grid. Only parking lots to puke in and wretch your toxic memories. Wash them off, watch the surrounding grass grow despite yourself and the strangers singing your name or dying in your back seat.

I looked at Officer Chad Carr across from me at Julie's small table. His starched police uniform looked respectable.

"The thing is . . . Marius hated needles. They horrified him. He never would have touched one no matter how drunk he got."

He looked at me, took a pause. "What are you saying, Bjorn?"

"What do you think?"

"Tell you what . . . let me talk to the medical investigator from Marius's file. The fact that they performed an autopsy on his body means they weren't completely certain about something. The toxicology report was sped up, maybe curiously. Or maybe just because they were dealing with a public figure." We were silent for a time. "I don't know why you guys were always so into drugs anyhow," he said.

"Probably the same reason you are so into working out and running after strange."

He didn't say anything.

I ate some kolaches, a donut, drank coffee excessively due to agitation. Carr's acknowledgment of what I already knew made me now mentally confirm the worst. I thanked him for meeting me.

"Say hello to the wife and kids."

"Yeah . . . thanks. Tell your old man to fuck off or go easy on his liver." He smiled. I smiled.

He looked at me with that 'stache. "You okay to drive?"

"I am okay with it if you are okay with it."

"Eat another kolache, dickhead," he said.

#9

Leonard was awake when I rolled in to his place, still in his underwear on the couch. He looked awful, like the bloated skin of his face had been grated.

"Where you been? You put gas in the truck?"

"Ask you something, old man. What do you remember about last night?"

"Got drunk. Walked home." He shrugged, made a simple face.

"Are you insane? Look around ... broken furniture. Shit everywhere."

"No harm done. None of this is worth nothin'."

"Sure. No harm done. That's right."

"Why are you so sensitive?"

"You got it. *I'm* hypersensitive ... put on some clothes. We need to take care of a few things."

There is no use in rationalizing with an alcoholic. They either possess self-awareness or they don't. They either remember or they don't. Leonard just doesn't, not much anyhow, and that won't change.

"We going to breakfast? I need food," he said.

"In a little bit. It's already the afternoon. I want to do some thinking first. Put on some pants."

"Okay, but I'm going to grab a couple beers."

Surrounding the Menil Art Museum and Rothko Chapel, close to the Seedy Café, was a series of one-story gray houses with white trim around the doors and windows. Many dark SUVs were parked in the streets, and an attractive middle-aged woman, smoking a cigarette and reading a book, sprawled on a bright red blanket in the museum's grassy park. A man swung on a wooden plank hanging by two ropes from an oak, and I asked Leonard if he wanted to enter the museum real fast to look at some paintings. "It's free to get in," I said.

"No, no," he replied, lighting a cigarette and opening a Lone Star. The woman in the park took her shirt off to uncover a bikini top. "You go. I'll stay here and enjoy the ambience."

"I'll only be five minutes."

I felt the past's shadows as I raced past Picasso and Max Ernst to the Rene Magritte backroom of the museum to stand before impressive light.

In front of me my favorite painting: a massive blue-white-gray depiction of a celestial boulder, egg-shaped and balanced on a mountain ridge with fading sky behind — titled "The Glass Key" after a book. To my left a painting of a window showing clouds instead of glass and darkness instead of sky; to my right a sky that was raining men in raincoats; behind me inside a house, another boulder, behind it an ocean view and thunder sky; but this grey light blue boulder on the mountain ridge is where I've always wanted to go; the glass key, where can I find it, where the casual sadness meets the sunny snow? Where a clear sky feels soothingly emotional? I longed to hug and sing to that boulder; up close, Magritte's mountain looked like it was melting. I wanted to save it, or at least find that sky. Find that cosmic unlikely, who knows where, any place to feel more whole. I took a can of Lone Star out of my pocket and opened it. Magritte and Lone Star is all . . . "Sir, there are no open containers allowed in the museum."

"It's just piss water," I said to the museum's security guard who wanted me to leave.

"Pound it," he said.

I did.

After my Menil fiasco, Leonard and I sat on a bench smoking cigarettes and sharing the last beer in front of towering bamboo behind an obelisk sculpture in the middle of a small pool next to the Rothko Chapel — Mark Rothko's windlowless spiritual octagon of brick and non-denomination.

A private Catholic college was a block away, and a woman sang a melody while playing a mandolin on the side of the pool's reflection.

"Very nice," Leonard said.

"Not bad," I said. "Let's go inside this chapel, get our minds right."

"Hmmph," said Leonard, putting out his Marlboro. "I guess."

Inside the chapel was as I had remembered it too: sparse, dim. Several large darkly painted canvases on its eight walls, only slight light coming through slits of the octagonal opening at the top. I sat down on a small round cushion on the stone floor, put my hands on my knees and my head down, then looked up to a vast dark canvas, my back turned to people sitting on benches where Leonard was.

I contemplated the presentation of, well . . . homicide. . . of a best friend who had been murdered.

The quiet.

The Phalanx rarely had quiet . . . neither did I. But this chapel. I remember my friend, the grin, the simple genius of it, the timing of a laugh.

To meditate is to clear a mind, but I don't want to clear it. I want to bring back my friend, share some of this quiet even messiness with him — at least understand how he departed or ask the earth why, try to find some god in a dark canvas, maybe feel the fibers of cushion on my back and try not to question a thing.

A thing. I talk to the moon even though I'm indoors: *God, you motherfucker, why take my friend?*

No need to ask.

Yet I ask.

My body went fully numb alongside the silence. I was in a clichéd film, a bad movie maybe; the drug overdose of a minor celebrity? But this had happened. This was happening. My senses were totaled, I hadn't hardly slept in three days, and my head was humming — and in all directions the canvases loomed. The light came through the modest slits at the apex of the chapel's octagon. As the story goes — as he was haggling with architects before the chapel's completion, Mark Rothko committed suicide in his New York studio in 1970.

I guess I should ask now:

Did Rothko actually kill himself?

I heard Leonard murmuring and shifting around on a bench against the back wall, and I looked up and behind at him; he made a shrugging motion with his shoulders and arms and then gave a look of discomfort, like he needed to get out of his shirt.

I pointed at the door, watched him go.

My face then back down in my hands, and I guessed I didn't need much more. I know what's here, this bit of light coming through the octagon for more than half the day in Houston. Don't need much more. No need to ask. No one ever comments on the grey walls of the Rothko Chapel behind the dark canvases. And after getting up from the cushion, I noticed a bearded kid with stocking cap, though dead of summer, take my place. He pushed the cushion a few feet over to sit exactly in the middle below the canvas for perfect equanimity.

Which had never occurred to me.

Outside the chapel the day was very hot, like a tomb; Leonard with his bear-toad body stood in front of the reflecting pool, sweating ferociously into it — a Hallmark card gone to grass.

"Why'd you leave?"

He shuddered, looked uncomfortable again. "'Bout as awkward in that chapel as trying to take a piss with an erection while sitting on the toilet... that was *not* what I expected."

"You mean you've lived in this city all these years and you've never been to the Rothko Chapel?"

"I mean it's just a bunch of nothin'. Some nothing paintings, few benches. I thought it would have more than that."

"That's the point. It's simple and universal. Just enough for everybody to reflect, maybe meditate."

"*Meditate?* Shit, boy. That ain't for me. It is *not* for everybody. What are we doing here in this heat? Let's go to the bar."

"It's just that..." I started to explain to him that when The Phalanx and I were in high school, when we couldn't think of much else to do, we would come to this museum area for what we called the *trifecta*: Magritte, Lone Star, Rothko; three legends and a soothing ritual for two dumb broke kids. I had vowed to come to these personally sacred places whenever I returned to the city, but ultimately I wasn't surprised that Leonard didn't want to look at paintings nor sit alone with his thoughts. "Never mind. Let's go to the Lotus, get you that breakfast then your liquid lunch. I called Mike this morning and he's arranged for me to meet a guy named Harrison."

"Read my mind," Leonard said. "Harrison could be Harrison Ford for all I care. At least the Lotus has more than benches. I'd like more than piss water Lone Star."

With added light and hangovers, the Lotus Tree during the day is a different beast. Quiet, bright, nearly tame, you're more likely to notice the worn-out nature of the place. The daylight rips in the backs of red chairs.

Leonard and I settled in, and Mike was glad to see us. He introduced me to a guy, very fit-looking, who was sitting at the corner of the bar.

This guy looked like he had zero body fat — tree trunks for legs, slight upper body in a tight chic grey suit, skinny black tie, hair gelled to a follicle, even though it was summer and a leisure afternoon. This was Harrison, he being of course also a professional soccer player who mostly rode the bench as a substitute with The Phalanx.

"Hello, Bjorn. I've heard a lot about you. Marius always wanted us to meet."

"I've seen you play. You're one hell of a stopper in the back."

"Not playing very much ... but thanks, I appreciate that." He tapped his fingers on the bar and glanced at his reflection before turning back to me. Listen, Mike told me some things you told him, and there's something else you need to know."

I listened.

"Marius was into some petty bullshit. I told him to forget it, but he paid no attention."

"Was he running drugs?" Leonard asked.

"Shut up, Leonard! Please. This is important."

Leonard held out his hand to Harrison to shake. "Boyd Leonard, pleasure. Buy you a drink?"

"No. I don't drink. Water's fine." Here's a guy that was nothing like The Phalanx. He was polite but kind of arrogant-looking, acting, even though I wanted to like him. And I also realized how ridiculous it was that The Phalanx was able to be a professional athlete while abusing his body the way he did. "So Marius was working with that strange guy Lee Roy, you know — the manager at that Greek café, The Parthenon?"

"Lee Roy?"

"He's not actually Greek. Lee Roy would look to

Marius for tips on games. Nothing actually illegal — just when players had nagging injuries, when they were likely to have good games and bad games. Who had a head cold or maybe the flu, who was having issues with the team or the coaching staff. Who was off at a certain time for personal issues, or weren't going to play well. This is a big thing right now in sports betting, especially with the big money in fantasy leagues. Any insider information that might help in placing bets for or against the team, even a particular player."

"Like a damn horse race," Leonard interjected.

"That's right," said Harrison. "Much like understanding the details for how any given horse is likely to perform."

"Probably making playback bets too," Leonard said it.

"What?" I asked.

"When you put cash on horses or games to mess with the odds for other bookies. Fairly common."

"That's right," Harrison said.

Leonard chimed again: "What did you say this Lee Roy's last name was, the non-Greek?"

"I didn't. But it's McCormack." Annoyed for some reason, Leonard turned and walked away to the far side of the bar.

"But Marius lost him a lot of money one game. A game against Kansas City. A bunch of the players were battered towards the middle of the season, and we thought the coaches were overtraining us even though they knew we were tired. We all knew we would lose to Kansas City, or at best tie them. I don't know if you saw that game, but Marius wasn't likely to play. Yet he came in as a sub in the second half and scored the winning goal with only a few minutes remaining in the game . . . we won that game 1-0."

"But why would Marius work with this guy? It doesn't make sense," I said.

"You knew Marius," Harrison said. "He saw the good in everybody. And you know he didn't use whatever money he got from Lee Roy McCormack on himself. He was always giving his money away to people who needed it. I told him not to do it." He tapped his fingers again on the bar top. "But here's the thing: It turns out he was doing a favor for someone who owed Lee Roy money."

"Who?"

"Just some stripper that owed him money. I forget her name."

"That motherfucker!" Leonard yelled. He was in the far opposite corner of the bar, smoking a cigarette.

"What?"

"That motherfucker, McCormack — the non-Greek! He's actually from Libya. I know his daddy. He runs some pipelines out of Baton Rouge!" Leonard pointed to himself. "*Petroleum* . . . as I know it, he was embarrassed by his dipshit son. Bought that café only for him to use it for pussy shit! I should have known: that piss-ant son murdered a man. The reckless son of a bitch!" He puffed out his chest, exhaled some smoke.

"Mr. Leonard, I'm sorry, but there is no smoking in the bar," Mike said.

"Goddamn right," said Leonard, to which I had no idea what he meant.

#10

I left the Lotus Tree and walked around Montrose alone — past some thrift stores selling loads of leather, pawn shops, burger places, other restaurants and overpriced antique shops on Westheimer, and stopped in at a dive bar called Conrad's.

Conrad's was The Phalanx's favorite Houston bar (where the pub crawl the night before should have started) — a usual middle-aged daily bartender named Guy with an orange mohawk and Buddha belly; a bare bones bar in a horseshoe shape, two TVs from the '80s, cheap drinks, a stellar jukebox and a tight side patio for smoking. Brilliant in its simplicity. Guy asked me what I wanted — "cheapest lager," I said — and he handed me a Lone Star.

The Karate Kid was playing on one of the '80s televisions above the bar. I proceeded to pound Lone Stars as Daniel LaRusso, a.k.a. Ralph Macchio, was getting his ass kicked by the leader of the Cobra Kai Dojo on the smoky beach at dusk at the beginning of the movie. After being hit and roundhoused in the face and gut several times, he lies head down hacking spit in the sand. As Daniel writhes disgraced and temporarily though painfully crippled, his so-called "friends" just decide to leave him there on the empty beach, as does Ali (played by the glorious Elizabeth Shue), the young woman who is responsible for getting Daniel's ass kicked in the first place. "They are just going to leave him there!" I yelled to Guy, "just bleeding and suffering on the beach!"

"People are fickle in California," Guy said. "If they were in Texas, one of his buddies would pull a shotgun out and make the Cobra Kai dicks beg for mercy."

"Goddamn right. No mercy."

"What, you've never seen this movie?"

"Mainly listen to music. Read paperbacks."

"Amateur," Guy said.

I continued to watch the classic movie and talk with Guy as I got more and more drunk, just amazed at how much abuse Daniel LaRusso was willing to absorb. After getting kicked out of the soccer team try-out at his new school, and having no friends and an annoying mother, he also has to deal with Ali's terrible friends who think he's a loser. He garners no justice until there's a Halloween party at the high school. Daniel, dressed as a polka-dot patterned shower with circular curtain to preserve his anonymity against said bullies, goes into the bathroom where he notices the main Cobra Kai d-bag, Johnny, in one of the bathroom stalls. In a moment of brilliance, Daniel puts a hose over the top of the stall, and turns the water on, which then drowns Johnny's skeleton costume make-up and soils the tiny joint of marijuana he is trying to roll while on the pot.

The scene commences with the Cobra Kai gang, all clad in spandex skeleton costumes, running after Daniel, as he jumps over a fence and hauls ass through a field. While he's about to jump over another chain-link fence that leads to his apartment complex, amid copious fog and menacing music, the Cobra Kais catch him and are about to make him *pay* once and for all.

"I've got it!" I said to Guy.

"What? You're about to miss Mr. Miyagi destroying these fascist karate jerks!"

"Doesn't matter! There's something I have to do. I need to go pour hose water on a motherfucker!" I put some bills on the bar top for Guy. "For my tab."

"Right on, Kid Vicious."

The Parthenon, Lee Roy McCormack's place, doesn't look like the Parthenon as much as a majestic modern Turkish smokehouse with symbolic Greek ornaments — pictures and sculptures of Greek statues, gods, and plebeians, a reproduced Athens and Instanbul.

Outside on the front porch, a young woman in black combat boots and black spring dress — another woman with a pink Japanese jacket with a scorpion on the back. Two people speaking Spanish and taking pictures of one another — a man sat next to me, shirt tucked in, wearing a tie, speaking into his phone. An older man with long hair looked like he could be in the Allman Brothers Band. Large green umbrellas over wooden tables, metal chairs. Ash trays everywhere, smokers everywhere young and old — wooden posts painted to look like old green and blue swirling marble. The Parthenon. I smoked a cigarette.

Inside, I could see no expense had been saved. Grandiosely polished wood everywhere. Marble counters and gorgeous chandeliers. Small white Greek statues on various shelves, Greek masks adorning the walls.

The decadent overhead of the place, no less a glorified coffee shop, screamed dishonesty. Fifty million cups of coffee couldn't pay for all this.

The jukebox played Frank Sinatra then a James Bond theme. Teenage girls in high skirts, college women in sweatshirts like '80s pop stars, business people on baby computers and laptops.

I walked up to the counter, noticing the quiche, lattes, mineral water — that atrium of wood — thinking too many laptops clash with wood . . . a silver platter with a stack of bananas — antique chairs of red and green pleather, weathered buttons around the seams. An escape, this oasis. I looked up at a framed picture of the Acropolis:

"The Erechtheion" read the caption. Who are these gods? The sound of the expresso machine — famous statue of a naked man with no hand. Art books on marbled tables low to the ground, wooden chairs. The woman behind the coffee bar asked me what I wanted, started to make my coffee, her back turned. "Is Lee Roy here?" I asked her.

She turned. "No. He's not."

Walking through the main room, I saw myself in the mirror as I went upstairs — long red beard pointing to the ground from the chin. Chains and rings, same white t-shirt for days. Burly, taller than most. The upstairs area had seating around the exterior, stain glass windows like a church. A large atrium balcony that looked down on the first-floor consumers, coffee and wood.

Amid that atrium with low wooden chairs before railings over the patrons below, what appeared to be a back wall was only an ornate cloth curtain to walk through.

Behind the curtian sat a small lithe man around an elaborate wooden desk in a room. The desk itself looked like it had been designed for a high-powered ambassador. His window looked out to the roof of a neighboring antique shop; a television in the corner flashed a screensaver of what looked like a tribe of Indians in the desert.

"Lee Roy?" He raised his eyebrows above expensive red-rimmed eyeglasses. "Let's talk about Marius Malanx."

Occupying a plastic kind of regality, he gestured for me to sit down.

"The thing is, Lee, he was found overdosed with a needle in his arm, and Marius couldn't stand needles."

He had that type of smooth skin that ages quite well — and a head of thick black hair even though I took him for middle-aged; his collared shirt was too big for his body.

He slowly stacked some papers into a folder, closed it and looked at me. "How is this my concern?"

"From what I understand you were unhappy with him. He cost you a lot of money. Maybe you wanted to punish him somehow."

He mashed the knuckles of his right hand down on the folder. "Kid, I have no idea what you are talking about."

"I am twenty-six years old. I think you do know. There are some associates of mine that have a lot to say about you. You and your father in Baton Rouge."

"*My father?*" He laughed a little then fingered his temple with his right hand. "I think you should leave. On your way out get another coffee to go — free of charge. The coffee here is excellent, best in town."

I took a drink of the coffee I already had. "I am not going to leave sir until you have explained how my friend has died."

He placed both hands on the desk, then folded his arms and leaned back in his chair. "Let me explain something to you, kid. You know the history of the American Indian?" I nodded. "The American Indian, the *Native Americans* as they call them these days, what's the consensus? That they were peaceful people. *Spirit* people — of the earth. *Of the earth?* Incorrect. They knew how to massacre. To *massacre*. To take what was theirs. I am not only speaking of the Europeans they battled and killed, no. I am also speaking of the other Native Americans. *Each other.* Their sense of justice was to butcher the top of your head . . . . if you deserved it. You understand?"

"That's a very convenient historical fantasy you've constructed for yourself," I said.

Lee Roy McCormack's eyes got huge. He fumbled past the stack of files on his desk and started to reach for his smart phone. A lumped mass barreled through the curtain.

Bear-toad Leonard with a shiny revolver.

It looked as if it had never been used.

"McCormack, you little non-Greek pussy! This boy deserves an explanation about his junkie friend. You don't give this to us I'm going to shoot your dick off, use your lips as a bun while you suck on your own bloody prick!"

I took his phone and threw it against the wall.

Lee Roy coughed, raised his hands slowly in the air. He looked shocked enough, but whatever fear he possessed was blanketed by fragments of familiarity.

He put both of his hands down on the desk. "It's true that your friend cost me a good sum of money. But it's also true that he lived a life of what you could call . . . *immoderate*." He now raised both arms higher for the whole world.

"Bullshit. He wasn't suicidal."

"Perhaps his death was an accident," he said.

Leonard walked over and slapped him. Lee Roy's glasses fell off his face.

"Don't make me call your daddy, son. Make me explain to him about his piss-ant son. Though my understanding is that he knows it already!" Leonard slapped him in the face again.

I had to halfway laugh. Lee Roy put his glasses back on. They were crooked.

"Please. You think I am not going to remember this intrusion? You think, fat man, that these threats are going to go unnoticed? You know what happens to a pig that walks into a butcher shop?!" He brought his arms down on the desk. Made two fists.

Leonard grabbed the guy by the hair, put the barrel of the gun to his lips.

"Open that Gaddafi mouth."

Half of the metal penetrated as Lee Roy gnarled

a mutter: "My father is half Syrian, half Scottish, you fat clown. My mother is from New Orleans, where I was born and raised."

"Listen here. We are going to make sure you show penance for what you have done. You can bet your desert whorehouse on that."

Outside on the sidewalk, Leonard looked pleased with himself. He took a drink from my cup of coffee, spit it out.

"This shit tastes like mud."

"What the fuck, Leonard?"

"*Fuck nothin'*. What do you think you were going to do in there? You think he was just going to calmly confess murder to you? By any broke dick's count besides, if he's responsible he's probably only barely responsible. These goons have other goons that do things without much instruction at all. The goon behind the goon."

"What? Since when are you well versed in gangster protocol?"

"Gangster nothin'. I just know how goons work."

He took the gun out of his pocket and raised the barrel to his mouth. He pulled the trigger and a small flame shot out that he eyed like magic.

He took a cigarette out of his front shirt pocket, lit it with the gun fire.

"Jesus. That's a lighter?"

"Of course. You think I'd have a gun around? I'd of shot somebody by now — probably myself in the testicles."

"Let me see that."

I took the lighter, pointed it up into the air, pulled the trigger a few times. The flames came and went with the remaining daylight. Cars drove down Westheimer robotically in both directions.

"We never did eat breakfast," Leonard said.

"Jesus." I had *not* seen it all. But something. The small shit was piling up in the river, the snow, for

some poor sap to scoop it all up for minimum wage.
"How'd you know I came here anyway," I asked Leonard.

"Boy, you think this is my first rodeo?"

He pronounced this last word, surprisingly, in perfect Spanish.

It was summer time in Houston . . . and the headliners were on vacation.

#11

I wanted to be by myself, so I dropped Leonard off at Seedy's, took his crap truck around the city. And I finished what was left in the plastic bullet of cocaine.

It was so hot, the air conditioning did not make sense at that point, so I rolled the windows down and took my shirt off — drove about a half hour west on I-10 through the cement and artifice, the strip on top of never-ending strip of cheaply made small malls and fast-food places and chains and generic constructions.

The sun had set with little poetry.

When I was a kid I was in awe of the out-of-this-universe pink and orange-gold sunsets and moonsets in Houston, but like everything else glorious, I came to find out those hues were a result of pollution and waste pumped into the city's ether. Like Santa Claus. Like love, the fantasy has a cost.

I made the turn off for the large park outside the loop containing the soccer fields of my youth.

Field after field to my right and left lay outside the windows as I drove the main road. These fields reminded me of a simpler time. A game on grass, a ball, agreed upon rules and teammates I could rely on — a common collective purpose.

The Phalanx and I did get into some things before I'd left nine years before. We had a history of whenever hungry going to hotels, creeping up to the front desk and overhearing someone getting their room key — "Here you go Mr. Johnson. Room 202 . . ." — then using that name and room number to eat and drink all we wanted at the hotel restaurant.

We also had hats we had gotten at a thrift store with *Red Cross* on them, and we went to restaurants, usually around closing time, and asked managers if they had any leftover food for the Red Cross food bank. And time to time we shoplifted petty crap from gas stations; we broke into abandoned houses and houses for sale to dick around, smoke and drink, maybe attempt to ingratiate the girls we had brought. Towards the end of high school he drove his mom's used station wagon with bucket seats that faced the rear window that could be manually rolled down. We'd drive around, throw black cat firecrackers out the back, and then we graduated to shooting Roman candles out of PVC pipe into oncoming traffic. Finally we got our kicks with a potato gun firing water balloons towards strangers. We broke into the school over a holiday, didn't do much, except I managed to piss on the door of the room belonging to a health teacher I didn't care for. We stole a car one night, drove it around for a few hours until I got too guilty and decided to park it where we found it, early morning.

Regular deviance of bored Houston teenagers. Nearly harmless fucking around, though probably lucky we didn't get into serious trouble. I remember instigating most of this. The Phalanx only seemed happy to go along, not really caring one way or another probably. Soccer, beer, girls, stupid pranks; we spent our youth pretty cheaply, never participating much in the regular goings-on of the high school. He seemed to get along with just about everybody well enough though, in his hyper though nonchalant way. I mainly kept to myself.

After practice one time, when The Phalanx and I

were kids, we didn't have a ride back to the city, so we started walking on a freeway then a highway. The Houston traffic kept on. We didn't think to hitchhike because that was not what you did. We were hungry and walked into a fast-food taco place.

He was lanky then, tall for his age. I remember asking him how we were going to make it back to the inner loop of the city. Back to our homes.

"We could call our parents," he said. "But screw it. Your dad forgot to pick us up."

"He's probably drunk again," I said.

"Forget that, Bjorn. Leonard's a gentleman for the most part, but you can't rely on him. And I sure as hell can't rely on my mom. She's a shut-in, man. We got each other. That's it."

"It would be easier with a driver's license."

"It will get easier. We are going to get cars, move out of our apartments and do what we want."

I knew even then that it would never be that easy. We had no models for how to behave, no good advice for what to do with ourselves.

"What we need right now," he said, "are tacos. All we have is right here. *Today*."

Then The Phalanx did something I had not seen before but would come to expect from him. Call it an awareness perhaps. A virtue.

He leveled with the older kid behind the register. "Hey, man, we just got off practice. His dad forgot to pick us up. All I got is a dollar. If I go around to the back door, can you give us a few tacos no one wants or maybe ones that no one is going to miss?"

"I can't do that," the boy said.

The Phalanx took a napkin and a pen off the counter, wrote his name and phone number down.

"Here's my number. If you are ever in my area, which is Montrose, I swear to God I will get you some beer and cigarettes."

"Montrose?"

"My word."

"Let me see what I can do."

The kid delivered. He gave us two bags worth of tacos and burritos.

"These are cold," he said. "But they are free."

"Montrose," The Phalanx said. "Beer . . . and take this for coming through." He took out his dollar and handed it to him.

"All we got is this moment . . . and tacos," he said after the guy had gone back inside. This was a simple thing, but it embodied my friend. He made the best of it, somehow made everyone feel more comfortable. He always did this.

That Saturday in the early evening that summer, some games were going on at the park of my youth. The fields had grass but they also had dust and hard dirt patches from the pounding in the more congested zones of play — the same patches that left long bruises on your sides after falling. I thought about these kids playing in these fields. They would not get everything they wanted, they would be disappointed. Probably frequently. But every once in a while something will happen that will keep them going a little while longer.

I parked the truck and felt the nostalgia as I walked the grass and dirt of an empty field, saw the worn-out patches around the goals and center half line that was more rock and dirt than green; I felt the memories. Joggers went by. Babies in strollers. Dog walkers.

The birds chirped through the trees, cars on Clay Road to the distance, the trees some burned out beyond the fields and I saw a simpler time, a grander time when I found meaning in something so small, a game, some friends, happy cheering parents on the sidelines — I remembered sitting back there as a sweeper feeling right — all was right, something about the sway of the trees how the dust picked up the little white flowers fluttering a simplicity — a joy in the simple when the mind is right ... but I will never fully get my mind back there again; seen too much, drifted too much, hurt all along. The dust flows, and the dirt stays, but the grass needs to be greener on all sides. I leave this part of Houston as it is — I let it be and I move on and along off to something else in attempts to create a new joy and simplicity ... create a different time with my own flutterings and flowers. My own. Goodbye. I have let these memories go with you and the trees that did nothing wrong. Yes, I am hungover again; I am drunk again, but I am sane, and I am bound.

Leaving the park, returning to the urban core, I took some hits from a can of Lone Star and was struck again by the nondescript nature of the city. All the shit was just like any major American city. There is just more of it in Houston. More of the sprawl. How is a person supposed to call this his hometown? Is it only for the people in it? Is that what makes a home? The familiarity of people and buildings?

But I didn't feel home. I knew my way around. I understood the traffic and humid heat and lack of zoning laws, but I wasn't proud of it. The place was just what I had remembered, only getting bigger and bigger like a gross baby, and maybe that's the only requisite for calling a place home. You can see if your memories match up or add up to what it has turned into. Driving around, I didn't know what this place was. Only associates for passing snapshots.

I stopped off at a gas station, gave a guy a dollar to use his cell phone and decided to call Merle. She was making dinner at her place and wanted me to come over.

I listened to tapes. Songs by the bands Lucero

and the Drive-By Truckers came out. As did a tune by Waylon Jennings about moving on with it:

> *Now I was goin' and if I'm goin'*
> *I'd better be gone*

I took the exit off the 610 loop and down Westheimer, avoiding the chaos around the Galleria Mall, past the large houses of River Oaks and the trendy high-rises of Upper Kirby. More of the same. Just more money put into it. I turned right off Westheimer onto Shepherd Drive into Rice Village and Merle's house, a glorified bungalow duplex on a tree-lined street priced at, I am sure, an unbelievable amount. I guess preaching about film at a university does pay . . . I breathe out and the film strip moves along . . . Waylon knows — the *goin'* and the *gone* are synonymous.

Houston: a place to drive.

#12

Her kitchen was a mess. Merle was a good cook, even if a consummate vegan, but her kitchen etiquette was lacking. The space looked like it had been raided by a SWAT team. Ingredients everywhere: hummus, tahini, lentils, dripping black beans, remnants of strewn vegetables exploded — in the sink, on the countertop, the floor. If Sid Vicious and Nancy Spungeon had a cooking show, this is what their kitchen would have looked like. Though I couldn't see any feces or vomit, no toilet heroin water to speak of; a punk rock song was playing, however, on low volume.

"Hi, Merle." I pointed behind me and realized how drunk I was. "I let myself in."

She turned. "Hey." Wiped her hands on her apron. "You hungry? I am making a quinoa and broccoli casserole. Some vegetables and hummus there on the table. Homemade."

"Homemade vegetables?"

"Hummus, jackass."

I sat down at a chair at the table. "I'm not sure about eating. I don't have much of a stomach for it."

"You should eat something." On the wall above that kitchen table some framed poster of a John Waters movie poster, an obese woman in drag, looked down at me.

"Been driving all day. All people do in this city is drive."

"Look at you, man. You look terrible. You want to take a shower?"

"Driving and consuming and sweating . . . no. I am reeling in my own filth."

"Dramatic."

"When does Dick Cinema get home?"

"Soon. When he gets here I don't want any bullshit from you, alright?"

I looked at her. Her apron, white and spotted like a cow's hide but with fake blood all over it. "I can't make any promises." That poster.

"The problem with you, Bjorn, is you carry this weight around. I don't know where it comes from. You need to let it go." She retied her apron. "You should read about the Baha'i faith."

This annoyed me. What the hell did she know. "This weight around? I think I have plenty of reason to feel this way . . . act this way." There was now a tension in that kitchen. "My friend has been murdered. *Murdered*. what does Baha'i have to do with anything?"

She kept looking at me. "You know I understand. But you can't let it add to the bullshit . . . to the damage of it all." I dipped a slice of green pepper into the bowl of hummus.

"The damage . . ." I heard the front door, and a man walked into the kitchen — kind of short, balding; he had a gut but was muscular. I could tell he overcompensated for his physical deficiencies. I did not like him or his visible core. A piss-poor aura. And I am not a Baha'i.

"More vegetables I see," he said.

"Vance, this is Bjorn. He stopped for dinner." He didn't shake my hand and sat down in the chair across from me, and we ignored each other for what seemed like a few minutes. "The ex-boyfriend," he said finally.

"That was a long time ago. One of many I'm sure." I fingered some chopsticks on the table.

"Not many get mentioned."

"Guess I'm lucky." This guy was a joke.

"What are you doing here, Bjorn? What kind of name is *Bjorn* anyway?"

"My parents are Mexican . . . Merle invited me for dinner."

"So I've presumed."

"Well if you've *presumed* then why are you asking me so many fucking questions?"

Merle interupted, "Okay you two, you're like a couple of middle school idiots. Let's eat dinner."

We began to settle in for dinner but Vance continued with his smug, snarky comments and I continued to act overly defensive and on guard like an asshole.

"So you've returned to your congenital state?"

"Vance!" yelled Merle.

"It's okay," I said. "Something like that. I do see a bunch of protruding genitals around here. But anyway we dated in high school, a long time ago that's true . . . she slept with a guy at a gas station. Some older guy." I pointed four fingers at him. "She likes older men."

He grinned.

"Wait a second . . ." Merle started.

"No, no, it is fine. Bjorn here wants to illuminate the past." He looked at me. "You like ruminating on the past do you, Bjorn?"

I picked at a carrot. "Is that casserole ready yet? I've always wanted to eat a casserole with chopsticks." Merle got up to look in the oven.

"You know what your problem is," Vance stated. "I can already tell. You don't know how to wait."

"*To wait?*" I looked at Merle who said nothing, standing by the stove. "I know how to wait for you, asshole. I know how to wait for a fucking casserole." I chopped the air with the sticks.

"I don't think you do. I think you lead with impulse, like a sophomoric jellyfish constantly trying to suck the ocean."

I stood up from the table.

"The problem is, you understand," he said, standing up himself. "The jellyfish is comprised of mostly ocean water. He seeks the very substance he is. Destroys it even."

"You are quite the marine biologist," I said. "I thought you taught film."

He grinned and leaned in closer. I could see a gap between his front teeth. That bald head. He was kind of frumpy but all ego in a pompous blaze of academia. "Film *is* biology. The anatomy of the entire world." I stepped closer to him. "What are you doing here, anyway? You and Merle hoping to have a threesome? Merle here likes a good threesome, don't you Merle?"

"Vance, goddamnit!" Merle shouted.

I badly wanted to punch this guy, rip into his organs with the chopsticks.

"You going to revert to violence now, Bjorn?"

"I am thinking about it."

"Violence is only for the weak-minded. The uncreative and inarticulate. People who cannot use words effectively resort to violence out of dullard frustration."

I stepped closer to him, looked him in the face. He had these pale blue eyes that I hated. He looked like he was capable of far worse than killing a man. You could tell he was the sadist type — the type who blew his wad to other's pain. "No . . . you have it wrong, professor. It's all communication. What I might say conveys the same message as if I punch you in the face. Punching you in the face conveys more probably, actually. This is what academics and so-called intellectuals don't understand. You can talk and talk, spew your pedantic bullshit, but in the end all you guys want to do is jerk each other off or wrestle around like girls on spring break in a mud pit." He started to say something before I took

Leonard's lighter gun out from underneath my shirt. "No," I said. "Verbal. Nonverbal." I waved the lighter and the chopsticks. "It's all communication. Sit back down, Vance."

He looked terrified of course. Merle screamed: "What the fuck, Bjorn!"

"No problem here. I was once told to always know a man's credentials."

"What the hell are you talking about?!"

I pointed the lighter at Vance, then pointed to my temple. Then back to him, held it there aimed between his eyes.

I shifted the gun to the bowl of vegetables, pulled the trigger. "I just thought you might like your vegetables roasted."

Vance started to cry, to weep quietly yet uncontrollably. I tapped the lighter on his shoulder. His face was down in his hands on the table. "Your sobbing is the most effective communication I've seen from you yet, professor."

Merle grabbed me and pointed to the door. "Let's go," she said.

As we walked towards the door, I noticed the flat-screen television in the living room. I broke away from Merle, picked up the TV and launched it into the coffee table. The glass shattered on wood, turning pixels into spider webs. "Put this in your fucking film!"

Outside, in the driveway, Merle let me have it. Yelled at me about my attitude, my behavior. Explaining that I couldn't treat people this way. Though I don't think she cared about the TV. I tried to convey to her that this Vance was no good, that she was wasting her time. She didn't completely disagree but she was hysterical nonetheless. I stopped her rant after she had gotten most of it out. "Are you coming to the viewing tomorrow?"

"Of Marius? Of course I am," she said, wiping her eyes.

"Sit down." I motioned to the grass to the side of the driveway. We both sat cross-legged facing each other. She was attractive. "Okay," I said. "Tell me what's really wrong with me."

"You dwell too much on horseshit, man! And you have to stop trying to change people, Bjorn, or at least stop getting so upset that people aren't the way you want them to be!"

"I just say what I know."

"Well, I got news for you. *Everybody* knows *something*. You're not the only one!"

"Sure." I got up off the ground, stood over her.

"What the fuck, man? How many places have you lived since you left here?"

"A lot."

"Yeah, why?"

"No reason. I am just trying to get on with it."

"You don't want to confront anything."

"Nothing to confront." I lit a cigarette with the gun lighter.

She was still sitting down in the grass. "Do you know why I hooked up with that guy from the gas station in high school?"

"Free cigarettes?"

"You had one foot out the door! You were already gone. I knew you would never stay around." She stood up, took off her apron, threw it into the grass. "And you still won't stay around!"

"Sure. But you didn't have to sleep with a guy at the fucking 7-Eleven."

"I didn't sleep with him! That was a rumor."

"Then why did you apologize?!"

"Because you looked like someone had died . . . kind of like you do now, and I felt really bad for you. You made it seem like there was no difference."

"You didn't sleep with him?"

"No, you idiot! We were stoned and I made out with him. But I didn't let it go further than that."

"Sure."

"Christ, man, I was only 17 . . . and do I have to say it? I found you half dead with slit wrists in your bathtub!"

Jesus. "I was only experimenting. I wasn't trying to kill myself."

"That's bullshit and you know it! . . . You just don't know a good thing . . . if it were planted on your fucking forehead!" Her head looked twice its size. I could see her bloody apron in the grass.

"Sure . . . I am just *swimming* in good things. That's right, self sabotage . . . bullshit." The truth is, as Leonard was passed out in the next room, I had slit my wrists the wrong way in the bathtub — more bloody than deadly. Merle found me, was so hysterical that I blew her off, and afterwards I walked to a gas station and got drunk on the sidewalk.

"That's right." She took my cigarette and held it in the air like a torch.

I looked at her in the grass. "Look . . . sorry about your boyfriend," I said before walking down the driveway into the neighborhood — into those ubiquitous ungodly oak trees that embraced me like a great aunt into her prodigious bosom.

Merle screamed after me. "Let it all go, Bjorn! It's not worth it!"

Let it go? Bullshit. I have wide eyes for my own shit in the toilet. Life is a shit river. *A shiiit rivaaaaar!* We can drive and drive. Eat, drink, shit until we think what was bothering us has passed with the flush of elaborate indoor plumbing and receptacles for waste that most don't see. Roar that damn air conditioning until you can't smell the funk.

Spray some freshener to help you pretend it doesn't exist.

I let nothing go. The past lives in me, creeps out

of my pores. It's not about intentionally dwelling in it, that doesn't matter. Despite all of our good intentions and protestations, these moments revisit us, in our memories, in our dreams. The shit resurfaces. The particles. *In our water.* I can't let go of the past so long as I don't want to let go of my arm or my foot. The past comes and the past duplicates. A sad repetition mostly. We can delude ourselves, say we have moved forward. But there is no moving forward. Not really. There are only present reminders and extensions. Present circumstances that bleed into those memories like a fucking jellyfish in the ocean. The ocean stings itself.

A fucking girl named Merle.

And The Phalanx. The goddamned Phalanx. A needle in his arm didn't kill him. We all did. Buildings included. With the underground air-conditioned tunnels as a vulgar swindler's replacement for right behavior aboveground during the clear and natural light of day. A goddamned collective concrete crucifixion.

And that's right, motherfuckers:

I am my father.

○○○

Sunday

"I had that feeling once. I was riding my motorcycle in northern California, stopped off where the land met the ocean. Everything was one, call it God . . . in everything. Everything perfect all in one. That's the feeling. That's the memory. Your memory. My present."

— **Marius Malanx,** *high*.

#13

I woke up on the side of a dumpster.

I had left that duplex in Rice Village and walked — bought a small bottle of bourbon at a liquor store and spoken to the moon:

What are the names of these monstrous trees? Do you want to punch me in the face? Are these perfectly manicured lawns outside reality? What is a village? Where is the time, and how has it been spent?
  Drinking. Living excessively, no plans really. Little purpose. I told Merle last night I just want to get on with it, but that isn't exactly true. The better truth is I don't know how to live. Not fully. Never had a career counselor, no guru — and I slept through the after-school specials. Education and career and family and potential — these dreams feel like cartoons, like a bingo game that other people play. Never had a clue, never had structured desire for what I want. How I want. Never been to AA, but the day-to-day living seems fine. Without dreams and goals means you live life without fantasy or delusion. You don't lie to yourself, but that's also a sobering way to live. There's a strange emptiness to that life too.
  That night after Merle's in Rice Village I had walked down Shepherd through Montrose, turned right on Alabama and kept walking east, still talking to the moon — turned left on Scott close to Texas Southern and the University of Houston,

headed north past small houses in disrepair and
government subsidized complexes. No one
bothered me as I spoke with the moon, yelled at
myself.

They could have.

They had every right to be angry living in these
Second Ward and Third Ward houses with broken
windows and busted foundations. Men old and
young standing around rusted cans and talking
and smoking and listening to music as I walked by.

It was too hot for trash fires, but people huddled
together underneath a couple freeways for shade,
as I then walked past sprawling abandoned lots
behind barbed wire fences maybe only Houston
has.

I continued past quiet houses and loud houses,
drunk and angry and prayerful. Along one stretch
of highway a pile-up on one lane, the other lane set
to a crawl. As I got closer I could see the wreckage,
an SUV flipped on its side — a compact car's front
was smashed, a teenager lodged in front of it, and I
kept walking.

About twenty paces then turned back — I wanted
to see the scene with open eyes. They had cut
the seatbelts in the SUV, put an older man on a
stretcher — his nose was broken into a bloody
mess. I looked over at the kid crumpled in the
compact, already gone. He looked like an object
that had been rearranged, and I took a step closer
to understand.

"Sir, please step away from the area."

I asked the police officer: "What happened? How
did this happen?"

"Doubt the kid was paying attention. Probably
on his phone, texting, maybe drunk or both. Didn't
notice one vehicle, caused another one to flip . . .
now, please, step away," she said.

"I hate cell phones," I said.

A grotesque yet routine occurrence, car wrecks

happen every day, we understand the label of
rubberneckers — people can't resist the horror
show; they have to slow down and look at bloody
destruction, crippling devastation, but they don't
stop. Not to help. Not to actually comprehend. As
superficial entertainment they watch as they do
an ass-kicking or a war on television, a beheading
on the internet. They get their blood flowing, but
very little happens beyond that. Unless perhaps
it's their friend or family member in that car, you
at least feel the details then.

Eight miles later after Merle's place, one small
bottle later combined with all the other shit, after
seeing that wreck, maybe eight hours later, I woke
up next to a dumpster, gravel and dust in my hair
and beard — some slobber with dirt caked, and I
made sure everything was there, which it was,
including my wallet. No one needed what I had. I
had walked north and east to the Fifth Ward, what
people say is Houston's roughest neighborhood.
But it didn't appear rough to me that morning.
People left me alone, as they had the night before,
but then again I looked like a lunatic smelling of
vomit and garbage.

As I walked that night and howled at that
moon, the dredged memories went together. I
thought about washing dishes in Oklahoma City,
patronizing piss-poor punk rock shows; sleeping
with newly divorced women. And Austin.

In Austin after OKC, I was drunk the whole time,
learned how to play poker and go to bed with the
sunrise. And Providence. Rhode Island the smallest
state — bartending at some hip place that catered to
art school kids who threw elaborate parties in
Victorian mansions. And of course that frenetic
hedonism of Brooklyn, even sad Manhattan where
I once passed out on the subway, woken by a cop,
handcuffed and arrested due to mistaken identity.

Of course those mountains of Vermont that could

have been Austria if I didn't look too close — these stories and memories that mesh and overlap, my mind a rolodex of experiences that then mesh and overlap with the immediate reality, combining for a collection of moments in the existence I live in, momentary too — in walking and talking to the moon, passing out with a smell of garbage, needing advice, or anybody.

Nobody at all.

No, the Fifth Ward isn't a *bad* part of town. There are no bad parts of towns. Only people who have had bad things done to them, put upon them; only people in places who have been forced to accept and implement bad ideas they have been told are there for their own good. People and buildings make a place on the surface, but the negative feelings and ideas then perpetuate the reputation and labels, bad/good/in between the moon and garbage.

Repeat.

The dumpster that had served as a headboard for my dusty last night's bed was next to a mini-mart, an oasis in an almost wasteland, my own: sweating, disoriented, forlorn.

Inside the mart were three men, a skinny older guy behind the counter, a larger older man drinking coffee at a table, and another old guy at the same table who looked almost dead . . . the man behind the counter spoke to me right away as if we had known each other for years, in a whisper: "See that old man — he comes in here every day, scratches a ticket for lotto. Every day. He would love to win, get rich, but that's not what makes him happy. He is happiest when he is playing, *every day*. You have the look of someone who doesn't like to play." He laughed, grinned in a familiar way. "You were snoring, passed out beside my dumpster when I opened up this morning."

I looked at him. He was right.

Leaning in closer, he said, "You see this man? With the large coffee cup with photos of his deceased wife and daughter and grandson who live far away on it? This lonely man, thinking about what he has lost. He doesn't enjoy playing either."

He was right, but I still didn't say anything — only bought some chips and orange juice and coffee and cigarettes and beef jerky and sunglasses and Advil. "Just give me twenty dollars, call it even. Say it's for the lodging."

I nodded and gave him twenty-five. No use in talking to the moon or anyone else, not on Sunday.

Not hungover.
Not on Sunday morning.

#14

Are there differences between memories and dreams?

The Phalanx and I were at a bar called the Sip in Austin. The Sip, a stripped-down no-frills place with cheap drinks and a ping-pong table. I was trying to order beers at the bar when some pencil dick beef-neck came over drunk as a loon. He kept muttering at me, nudging me in the side fairly jovial but persistent in a way that was more than annoying. He took one dollar bill after another out of his front pocket and threw them down between my arms resting on the bar. He spat as he talked, a couple inches from one side of my face.

"I think you are getting too close," I said.

"*I'z justs tryto . . . buyyouz ah drinks . . . beez nye . . . ice.*" The slur and spit culminated; he edged up and nudged me again, so I pushed him back.

He took a swing at me but was too drunk — I kind of caught his fist, brought it down to his side, like we were playfighting. But he began to swing at me with his other hand, so I punched him in the mouth.

Watching this, The Phalanx then smashed a beer bottle on the top of the guy's head as he was going down.

Pretty gratuitous.

The owner of the Sip, a guy named John I knew from bartending in the area came over to us. "I saw the whole thing. And I understand, but you guys should probably leave."

The Phalanx helped the pencil-beef up to a chair at a table, gave him some water and a towel for his bloody head. In my car driving the guy to his house, he kept whining: "*Youz guys fucks me up . . . youz fucked me.*" We told him he would be fine, as we pulled into the driveway of his generic house in a suburban neighborhood on the north part of town.

"Wait here," The Phalanx said to the guy. I then saw him talking to some woman who had come to the door, presumably this guy's wife or girlfriend. She shook The Phalanx's hand and appeared to be laughing.

"You're good to go, Allen," he said. "I told your wife what happened. Get some rest, buddy. Take care of that head."

"*Fucks youz,*" this Allen said quietly as he got out of my car and stumbled up the path to his front door. He looked like a wounded animal as he did this — a gorilla or something that just wanted to lick himself in sad solitary defeat. He started to cry as he wrapped himself in his wife's arms.

"Not about the wreckage," The Phalanx told me. "About how you clean up the mess."

We returned to the Sip. I bought John some drinks for forgiveness while we talked. A DJ was playing punk rock and heavy metal music as people frenetically danced and slammed around.

The Phalanx started to dance with a woman, jumping about with the rest. But at one point he just slow danced with her, held her tightly, while everyone else knocked around like crazy, less-than-inspired people.

The Phalanx and this woman danced like that, slowly, for a good while — his head on her shoulder, the whole world blind.

And back in the car I asked him about it: "What was all the slow dancing about?"

"Sometimes it's best to slow it down. You got to be gracious, Bjorn. You got to be gracious."

I laughed at this then, lit a cigarette, but I've remembered. I remember these words now as if they were written on a small tablet or napkin. Call it a bible, a reminder for something.

Anything at all.

#15

I got a ride with some teenage kid to Midtown, then walked the rest of the way to Leonard's place in Montrose and collapsed on the couch.

He came out of his room and threw something in my lap. "Got you a breakfast taco, boy. You shouldn't leave town without eating a breakfast taco." I groaned, came to, felt my beard.

"Thanks . . . that was pretty nice of you." I looked at him standing over me like lumber. "There's some thoughtfulness left in you yet, old man."

"Shit, nothin'. No thought in it. Them tacos about the purest thing left in this world."

I took a glorious bite of grease and handmade tortilla. "Goddamn right."

"Where the hell were you last night?"

"Walking around."

"Where's my truck?"

"Outside Merle's place. Got too drunk."

"Can't relate."

We had a few hours until The Phalanx's casket viewing, call it a funeral, and after showering finally, I put on my jeans and the only button-down shirt I had. There was a decent moment there wherein Leonard gave me one of his ties, helped me put it on. About as father and son as we could get.

Walking through Montrose, Leonard asked, "Where we going, anyhow?" He took out that gun-lighter, held it in the air. "It's hot as shit."

I took the lighter back from him. "Midtown."

"Fuck, that's a long walk in this shit."

We rolled up to The Phalanx's condo, a large complex with a gate — dozens of similar-looking residences, two-level cookie-cutters. "Damn eyesore," Leonard said.

"I know. Can't believe he lived in a place like this." Several units — new, cheaply built, for the bulk of the yuppie Midtown growth. "But we need to get inside his place."

The door of the condo was locked of course, and it was too early in the day to break in illegally. "What are we going to do?"

Leonard scoped around, found an office towards the back of the 'plex that was closed. A guy in a blue workman suit walked past. "You work here?" I asked him.

"Yeah, you need something?" We explained our situation, about the death in one of the condos.

"I know all about that, and I'm real sorry, but I can't let you inside his condo though. Just not allowed, sorry."

Noticing the guy's name patched to the front of his work suit, Leonard remarked, "Look, Dick, can I call you Dick?"

"Richard."

"Yeah, look Dick, we need a favor from ya."

"Told you I can't do it. I'm just the maintenance guy."

"I'm a maintenance guy myself. *Petroleum*. So you actually run the place." Leonard laughed, pulled money out of his billfold. "Maybe we can make it worth your while."

"I don't take bribes." Leonard unzipped one of the top front pockets of the guy's worksuit, put the cash in.

"Not a bribe. Only a thanks. Can't imagine the square balls who own the place pay you enough."

This guy looked annoyed, pulled the money out of the pocket and handed it back. "Keep this . . . but you know, I'll let you in . . . but only because I knew Marius. I actually probably owe him money, tell you the truth." He looked down at his boots. "I really liked that guy."

I didn't say anything.

"Kind of squirrelly, but not a bad kid . . . just got too deep in the shit," Leonard said.

"I will give you ten minutes."

"One more thing," Leonard said, before stuffing the cash back in the guy's front pocket. "I noticed a camera for the place above the gate when we walked up. You still got footage for that?"

"I could lose my job for this."

Leonard took out more bills, stuffed them in Richard's front pocket. "For your rainy day fund. I don't reckon your boss is here on Sundays anyhow." Richard muttered something indecipherable then led the way to the back office.

I grabbed my old man by the shoulders.

"Here's what I got from that night, July 14th," Richard said behind a plastic desk in a small office with a modest box of black-and-white footage on an old television. "I've looked at it myself, and it doesn't mean much, far as I could tell. I told the police the same thing."

We watched the footage . . . and here's what I remember combined with a version of the notes I took:

> **11:37 p.m.** — *Lizzie, the woman I spoke with from the Emerald, walks out of the complex.*
>
> **12:02 a.m.** — *The Phalanx in a bathrobe comes in front of the gate. A woman who is clearly a streetwalker enters the picture. Phalanx gives*

her a hug, then pulls money out of his robe's pocket, gives it to her. The woman leaves and The Phalanx sits cross-legged on the sidewalk and lights a cigarette.

12:09 a.m. — *A drunk young couple come into the frame, staggering and waving their arms. He gives them a cigarette. Young guy gives Phalanx a fist bump. Young couple leaves.*

12:16 a.m. — *Another couple walks by, seem to be arguing. Phalanx gets up off sidewalk and speaks with them, hands in his pockets. Young guy appears to spit in the Phalanx's face while young woman yells at the guy. Phalanx gives her a cigarette then sits back down. Young couple leave.*

12:28 a.m. — *Another streetwalker, what looks like a homeless man, enters the frame. Phalanx gets up and gives the guy a cigarette, pulls out some money. The man seems to be talking nonstop, Phalanx only listening. The man takes a punch at the Phalanx, but Phalanx dodges it, turns around and sits back down on the sidewalk. The man says something, it looks like he is shouting, and then leaves. The man comes back into the frame and gives Phalanx a hug, then leaves again. The Phalanx lights another cigarette and after a while heads back inside, out of camera range.*

I didn't like seeing my friend alive again, especially not in soundless black and white. "I hope he had more smokes back at his condo," Leonard said. "What do you think, Dick?"

Richard turned the TV off and faced us. "Like I

said . . . this all seems pretty typical. This complex is right in the middle of Midtown, so it gets a lot of traffic from people leaving the bars and homeless loitering all the time. And Marius knew a lot of these street people and was always trying to help them out. They used to come knocking on his door all the time, until another resident complained to management and they put a code on the gate. So more recently you would see him meeting people on the sidewalk in front. Nothing strange about any of this, not to me."

"Besides blowing all of his money on addicts," Leonard said.

Jesus.

We're all addicts, Leonard.

#16

Up some stairs, the inside of The Phalanx's newly built condo was what they call minimalist, what Leonard calls *squirrelly*. "What is this? A Rothko thing," he said.

A futon mattress in the corner of the living room, one sheet and no pillow, a small lamp and a few paperback books beside; a narrow, low table made out of the side of an oak tree, crafted and polished; a few cushions around the table. The back bedroom was empty save for some clothes on the floor, and the small room downstairs next to the one-car garage only contained his vintage motorcycle. The bathroom had a bar of soap, two toothbrushes, an electric razor and product for that stupid haircut. In the refrigerator in the kitchen was a bunch of rotting vegetables and several bottles of lemon-lime Gatorade. Two large posters tacked crookedly to the living room walls; one of Townes Van Zandt (fellow Houstonian) in cowboy attire, another one a promotional for the film *Paris, Texas*.

I guess the cops had confiscated any drugs or paraphernalia.

Leonard opened one of the Gatorades, sat down on a cushion on the floor with an exaggerated groan, wiped his brow. "Hot as shit in here. Needs air conditioning." I knelt down to pick up two paperbacks on top of a stack next to the futon: a novel called *Housekeeping* by the writer Marilynne Robinson and another book named *Awakening the Buddha Within* by Lama Surya Das. I opened the Robinson, and on the blank back few pages was a dated list in The Phalanx's scrawl:

June 3ʳᵈ : *I met with Lee Roy again tonight. Strange to feel a man's body like that for the first time. This man needs help. What else can I say? The man needs . . . someone.*

June 9ᵗʰ : *I need a vacation . . . This season is killing me.*

July 11ᵗʰ : *It's been written that human beings are the cancer of the earth. I don't on occasion disagree with this. The best a person can do is attempt to be dormant cancer cells, one of the cells that does less harm to the body. This is what I try to be, I try to aid the other cells in doing less damage, and I want to inflict as little harm on the body, but at the end of the day I do sometimes still feel like a cancer cell. There has to be some other reason or purpose for human existence. Though maybe each of us has a chance to connect with something other, something larger or better — outside of this universe even, but certainly some thing or force or feeling beyond our five senses, beyond our cognitive comprehension, beyond the material we manipulate for our own selfish and self-serving desires and wants. Which relates somewhat to my compulsion to escape or check out from my regular consciousness with drugs and things. It is these times I feel humans are actually cancerous that I want to escape the most. I've even started injecting heroin, which I thought I would never do. The escape and feeling does work temporarily, but then when I come out of it I'm left where I'd started — which is then when I try to do all that I can for people, and* *probably if I am honest at least partially out of guilt, but maybe I should be doing more for the earth itself. I want people to feel less suffering — to be free to think, speak, and do what they want with meaning. That's the only reason to have money or anything else — to feel less constrained and reigned in. To ultimately break free of feeling cancerous or meaningless. But fairness doesn't exist, unfortunately. Only good intentions and reasonable actions, at best, with no guarantees. I don't know. Do I need to tap into something larger? Is that even possible? I know this: when I get through with this soccer journey, I am going to move to the mountains, find that boulder, buy some land. Any of my family and friends could live on it, as harmoniously as possible. Bjorn especially could use some healthy roots, some healthy positive grounding for his obviously tortured aimlessness. I want him to be more serious about the lightness, the goodness there still is. He needs the solid love of a good woman, and he needs a stable environment. He feels like a brother, a family member, but he also at times feels like my child. He represents who I hope to help. All of them do. Lanie and Tom and Delilah and Liz and Clarence and Harrison and Jeff and Boze and Janice and Lee Roy (maybe especially Lee Roy) and on and on and on and on <u>AND ON</u> ... I want to do better. We all can do better. This is what I want. This is what I yearn for. This is what I tell myself. One more hit, a few hours of sleep, try all over again tomorrow. Jump in tomorrow with no fear — with all of the grace in this world, and next ...* **MM**

TO DO, tomorrow, 14ᵗʰ:

Work out/practice.
Be kind. Give.
Call mom.
Stop doing junk.
JOY.
Go to Goodwill to get new golf driver.
Get more sleep.
Snag couple plants for condo.

July 15ᵗʰ: *Need a trifecta. Magritte. Lone Star. Rothko. Start with that boulder.*

I kept the novel and threw the other book written by a Long Island monk down at Leonard.
"Never heard of it," he said, and he threw the book back at me.
"Me neither." I lit a cigarette and walked out of that eyesore condo and Midtown and urban cancer and shit fuck-all what have you, the heat and humidity and endless maze of what-shit fuck-Christ, Houston, Jesus, now Buddha . . .

That's right.

River twice is a swamp.

#17

The days after The Phalanx died he got a few thin and narrow blurbs on the back pages of Houston newspapers. I still have a couple of them right here. I also notice the other headlines before and around his, many of them longer and larger:

NFL's Peyton Manning Retired . . .

    Crude Oil Up . . .

        The British Open Begins . . .

Houstonians Complain About Traffic . . .

"Obama in talks with Iran" . . . "Creative burgers were lighting up the Houston summer" . . . the U.S was playing in "Soccer Gold Cup" . . . a man got 30 years in a "fatal drug sting" . . .

"Record auto sales" . . .

"UN backs Jordan's claims on the site of Jesus' baptism" . . .

COMMENTARY: "International soccer scandal a cautionary tale for corporate sponsors" . . . Harper Lee in the news again with new book . . .

WINNING NUMBERS . . .

"Hole in Ones" . . .

BIRTHDAYS...

RETIREMENTS...

"New military monument off to rocky start"...

*Market summaries... News "In Brief"...
MLB All-Star Game... "Safety of air bags
questioned"... "Child drownings way down in
2015"... Data collected from Pluto... letters
written about religious freedom & freedom
of speech... Greece in turmoil... WINE...
TELEVISION...*

*"a 28-year-old woman committed suicide in
Houston jail"... "Crude Oil Down"... "Retail
giants clashed over prices"... "one of area's
major psychiatric hospitals shuts down"...
"Ted Cruz spars with New York Times"...
"Iphones lead in profits"... artic drilling...
"Mom out on bail after 3 kids drowned"... "Oil
Sinks!"...*

*"Train hits man who tripped, got trapped"...
"Confederate symbols under more scrutiny"...
"Pentagon plans to lift ban on transgender
individuals"...*

LIFE TRIBUTES...

*The Houston dog show... a father ran over his
son with his riding lawn mower... robberies...
burglaries... tax fraud... young workers at
Starbucks...*

*"Crude Is Down"...
BIRTHDAYS...
Bill Cosby...*

WINNING NUMBERS...

Market Summaries...Houston Astros...Rice University...
Boy Scouts...gray matters...El Chapo...

LIFE TRIBUTES...

housing prices...a high of 102, low of 88...

"Professional soccer player dies in his sleep"...

"Malanx Death an OD?"...

"A Thousand Gather to Honor Houston's Malanx"...

#18

Another story from Oklahoma City...

We were at a party at a house of the drummer or bass player, I can't remember which, of a pretty successful pop-rock band from the late '90s early 2000's. I would mention the name of the band, but they are terrible.

The house was pretty large and in a nice neighborhood of wealthy families, but the inside of the house looked like a teenager lived in it: a pool table instead of a dining room table, posters for movies instead of framed photographs of family members.

I have two memories from this party.

One: in the backyard was an aboveground pool. Next to the pool was a trampoline where people were drunkenly and hysterically jumping from the trampoline into the pool. I vividly remember one woman completely naked, with enormous boobs, bouncing on the trampoline and diving into the water.

Two: at one point in the night I had to piss, so I went into the corner of the large yard to go in the bushes and trees. As I was relieving myself, a small pug dog ran over and started lapping up my arc of urine. I tried to move my junk and stream away from the dog, but his little pug face just kept running side-to-side drinking my piss. As this was happening, a woman came running out the back of the house, screaming, "What the fuck are you doing to my dog!"

"There's a misunderstanding," I said. "Your dog was trying to drink my pee."

"What kind of terrible person are you?!" she screamed.

The Phalanx had witnessed what was happening and walked over and scooped up the pug. "What a great dog you have here."

"Thank you," she said.

"He must like vanilla cognac."

"What?"

"Vanilla cognac. Bjorn here's been drinking top shelf vanilla cognac all night so your dog must have a taste for the finer things. I bet if he had been drinking Lone Star your dog wouldn't want any part of this."

"What? Your friend was encouraging him. I don't see . . ."

The Phalanx started kissing the pug on the mouth. He stuck out his tongue and proceeded to French kiss the dog over and over again. They furiously licked the sides of each other's faces.

"What the hell?!"

"I think your dog and I are soulmates." He scratched the little pug's belly. "You little champion. What's his name, anyway?"

"Cornbread," she said.

He kissed the little pug on the mouth again. "Goddamned Cornbread. What a gentleman." He held out his hand to the woman. "Marius."

She tentatively smiled back and then started laughing. "Well, fuck me. Y'all want to get in this pool?"

Eventually, after swimming and watching the sunrise with topless ladies, we walked away — away from those titties and the yard and the water above ground — back to the sidewalk to get breakfast burritos from a 24-hour Whataburger, about as close to Texas you can get in Oklahoma.

So it goes.

#19

The last time I saw Marius "The Phalanx" Malanx, he punched me several times in the face.

In Vermont. I had a few days off, so we played a pick-up soccer game on a lush field next to a mountain with the Stowe locals. I sat back and played defense because I hadn't sprinted in a decade, and The Phalanx scored about nine goals in fifteen minutes.

The locals were thrilled.

Back at staff housing, we sat in lounge chairs on the back patio overlooking the grey mountain and drinking beer. "So this doesn't seem so bad. Bartending in the mountains?"

"For rich people," I said.

"Yeah for rich people. Why do you always have to find a negative?"

I finished my beer, opened another one. "I'm just saying. Bartending in the mountains is great. I just don't like dealing with rich people on vacation from Manhattan or wherever."

He laughed. "Better tips though."

"What do I need money for? I buy all of my clothes and books at Goodwill. I'm allergic to electronics — never buy that crap."

"Fine. That's pretty extreme, but do whatever you want to do. You know money makes me nervous too. Just do whatever you want with it. So we're all a bunch of weirdos. Who the fuck cares, man. Just embrace your inner weirdo. What the hell are you worried about all this shit for, Bjorn?"

"I have no idea."

"Well, where do you want to be?"

"Back in Austin maybe. Or Colorado."

"Then do that and stop fucking around . . . moping around. Pick a place to work that doesn't feel miserable. I plan on moving to the Rockies one day too. So do that — we can open a bar together and get drunk all day if you want and talk to people."

"Yeah right."

And then he punched me hard in the face.

"Ow . . . fuck! Why'd you do that?!"

"I wanted to knock that depressed look off your face. Look around, man! Enjoy your life. So you had a shitty upbringing with disappointing parents and other shitty jack-offs around. So did I! People aren't perfect, man; believe me. We can do what we want now. So do . . . whatever . . . the fuck . . . you want. And enjoy it! At least you don't have any kids."

"Do what we want? Jesus, of course we can do what we want. The problem is I don't know what to do. I don't have a fucking home!"

"Houston is your home, man."

"Houston?! Give me a break. Everyone I came up with there's still drowning in that ridiculous city that makes no sense at all. Anyway, who the hell do you think you are?"

He grinned. "I'm just the *midnight rider*, man."

"That's stupid and you know it."

"Whatever . . . just keep drifting around and enjoy the experience. Or build your own family or community elsewhere. It doesn't matter!"

"I don't know how! I never learned how to do that."

"It's easy, man." He lit a cigarette, smiled. "All you have to do is treat life like a dance."

"*A dance?* Jesus Christ, that's your advice?"

The Phalanx hit me hard in the face again.

"What do you want, a Zen Buddhist koan? All the clichés are true, dude: Live in the moment. Seize the day. When shit hits the fan, this too shall pass. The world is your oyster. Learn ... from ... your ... mistakes. Try to enjoy your life; try to be kind, or at least attempt to see the good in people. Don't sweat the small stuff. Treat life like water because it *is* water. There ... is ... no ... ideal. Always treat nature like you've been in the desert for years. Or ... pretend every human you meet is the first person you've met since being in outer space for several years ... and the Golden Rule ... "

"Same shit, different day," I said.

"See what you did there?"

"Alright, punch me again."

He broke a bottle on my head. "It's like Janis Joplin said! You got one day, man! Don't worry about the goddamned other 364!"

And then we beat the shit out of each other.

Afterwards we sat back down, got even more drunk off Vermont beer, went to a bar and danced with a group of pleasant ladies on a bachelorette party from Montpelier who were wearing penises for hats. The Phalanx did the centipede, among many other signature dance moves, on the floor of the bar as people cheered.

Other life choices were made; we woke up the next morning and played golf in combat boots. Then we proceeded to pound beers, play pool and ping-pong, and listen to pretty solid music on the jukebox. Later that night I had relations with a cougar in a room at the resort. We ate room service off each other's bodies. The Phalanx spent the entire night dancing and getting drunk with strangers and swimming in the pool and lounging in the hot tub.

He slept with three women, and we both were hungover as shit the next day.

Well... Houston — *and* Oklahoma City and Austin and Brooklyn and Providence and Indiana and Vermont and... wherever else between... I do apologize. There were some good times in there too that I haven't mentioned. Sorry. As you know, depression fogs the windows. When you're down, you're down, and life gets confusing sometimes as you're trying to get out of it. With more time and sleep and relative sobriety though, I now better realize all of this. I've even started playing a little pick-up soccer under outdoor sun. Some snow without shit.

Life remains of course. And you got it: The goddamned Phalanx. That motherfucker was right.

About all of it.

I just wish he were still around.

#20

I took the Triumph from The Phalanx's condo to the funeral parlor, Leonard holding me around the waist and heavily breathing and talking nonsense behind me the entire time.

After parking the cycle, I lit a cigarette. "You go on in," I told Leonard. "I'll see you in there."

A few silent minutes passed before I noticed an old guy standing there next to a bench in front of the funeral parlor, smoking a cigarette of his own, looking as if the world was just fine.

He looked at me and pointed his cigarette. "I know you," he said. "You were in the cell with me a few days ago the night that boy died. He had those seizures and died."

I recognized him now. He was congenial, even in that cell. "Yeah, that was hellish. He died?" I scratched my beard. "Some kind of place away from reality that was."

He laughed. "Ain't nothing hospitable in that shit I tell you."

"No there isn't," I said. "Can't believe that was only three days ago."

"Shit, man, I just got out. I lost my entire damn weekend."

"This city."

He smiled almost laughed again and motioned towards what seemed like Midtown and downtown with that jail beyond, its bars, along with the highway and highrises and bounty of adult escapes in the distant periphery. "Any place is *confinement* if you want it to be. That is for certain." He turned back towards me, inhaled smoke, exhaled. "All the same . . . Houston ain't for those with no gag reflex."

"It sure isn't," I said.

He ashed his cigarette, pointed it at me again. "But there is joy in the gag I tell you . . . you remember that." I looked at him. "Never shave that beard, son. It suits you," he said.

"I will not."

"You got a dollar?"

I looked in my wallet, gave the guy twenty bucks.

The funeral parlor was packed, jammed with people inside and sprawled outside on the grass. It seemed half of Montrose was there. People of all types smoking, crying, laughing, sweating.

The parlor was a simple place off Westheimer, a modest brick house that had been converted; square patches of ivy around the front windows. A very tall and kind woman ushered us in, directed us towards a crowded room with rows of antique chairs. Expensive chandeliers hung down, and the walls of the main room were covered with wallpaper depicting an English countryside.

As on Friday night, there were countless people I did not know. But Merle was there, and so were Chad Carr and Mike, along with Harrison and a few members of the team — Hillary and Lizzie and Jackie, even Richard, some other fans of The Phalanx I now also recognized from the bars.

Standing in the hallway before the doorway of the room was an older woman in a black outdated dress, a far gone look on her face but still beautiful.

She recognized me and waved me towards her while sucking on an electronic cigarette.

"Mrs. Malanx?"

She took the cigarette out of her mouth. "This is just water vapor," she said, waving the cylinder.

"No nicotine. Trying to quit . . . it's better than nothing." I nodded and gave her a hug. She smelled like flowers. "Look at you," she said, patting my tie slowly. "Marius would approve . . . Bjorn, I am supposed to say something in there. I had planned on it. But all those people? You know me. I would just mess it up. Would you mind saying a few words about Marius for me?"

This woman's sorrow. She barely left the house and here she was. "No problem at all."

She smiled, gave me another hug.

"Victoria! How the hell you doing, girl?" Leonard as usual was inappropriately loud.

Mrs. Malanx breathed out, actually looked relieved when she saw who it was. "Well, Boyd, I can certainly complain."

He pulled her towards him for an embrace. "We will get through this," he said. "We will prevail through this thresher. The prodigal son here knows it too."

"Oh, Boyd. I wish I could believe you."

"Belief nothin'. We was young and now we are old. We always pull through, dammit. Come on now. Let me escort you to your seat."

He led her by the arm.

I sat in a chair in the front row, and, once everyone else was settled in, the kind parlor lady began her piece. "We are here for the departed. All of you . . . and there are so many of you, which is a testament in itself . . . all of you who knew and loved Marius . . . are here today to honor his life. And from what I understand, what a life it was. Such spirit.

"As you know . . . on behalf of the wishes of the family, a traditional funeral will not be taking place. The family has asked for an open casket. Very few cosmetic adjustments were made to the departed's body, as I understand he would have wanted it. Thank you all for coming. Please feel free to step forward, pay your quiet respects. Stay as long as you like.

"But beforehand I know Victoria Malanx, Marius's mother, would like to say some words... God bless you all."

Mrs. Malanx looked over at me, and I stood up in front of the open casket to face the crowd. In that moment I got a good look at The Phalanx lying there. His long blond half beard, that stupid haircut. He was wearing a grey suit I had never seen him in. He would have hated it. This wasn't him. His soul or whatever having left a good while ago. I reached into the coffin and took the tie off of him. "Sorry," I said, now taking my own tie off and putting both ties in my back pocket. "Marius wouldn't have been caught dead in a tie like this, and I'll be damned if he's caught dead with a tie like this now. Pardon me."

I looked at the crowd. Some were shocked but not that shocked. "Mrs. Malanx has asked me to say a few words on her behalf today. Excuse me." I felt the dry throat, the blur of my mind's eye, and knew I had to keep it together. "Where do I begin? Marius was a man. A good man, a decent person. But it was more than that. I called him my best friend even though I don't believe in the label of best friends. The best I can say is that Marius was the best person I knew at *being* a friend. He just was. And I'm sure many of you could agree with that."

I looked back at his face and exposed upper body in that uncomfortable suit. "Sure, he had that damn haircut, but he was more than a haircut. Even more than a professional soccer player." His one professional goal ran through my head — the ball flawlessly going through the sticks off his left foot, upper ninety — goddamned beautifully pristine. "Even though for a couple seconds there he was absolutely perfect at that ... He was ..." I paused, getting a bit choked up. "Well . . . he was . . . a goddamned gentleman. That's the best way I can put it. He was a gentleman. Sure, he was social and generally easygoing. But he had an intensity to him and a sensitivity; I know for a fact that he went through his own dark moments on occasion. And, sure, he liked to have a good time. Most of us do. And he had a propensity for escaping the world's shit every once in a while, as many of us here also do." A few nods.

"But he was a gentleman through and through. The kind they don't make anymore. He once said to me that he considered himself the *midnight rider*. I immediately told him that this was a ridiculous nickname." There were some laughs. "Sure, he liked to ride that cool-looking vintage motorcycle around like Steve McQueen or some shit, but I told him that the midnight rider is a cliché. Because the thing is . . . Marius was not a cliché. He was much better than that. A genuine person. One of the good ones. The more apt term, to use another song reference, would be to call him a *free bird* — a free spirit. The rules of the soccer field could barely contain him. Not many rules could. That dude did what he wanted, how he wanted, and we're all better off for it. He was a gentleman." I was starting to stammer and repeat myself. "Excuse me, Marius Malanx . . . I am better off for knowing you. We all are. Thanks for everything."

I looked out into this crowd of people and thought about them. And I thought about the hundreds more outside the parlor on the grass and the concrete. The people *loved* him. Admired him. And it dawned on me: No doubt he was dear to me, but he was dear to a *lot* of people. He gave himself — all of himself. He knew how to take the weight of the world and spin it back in a more rhythmic way.

"Because the thing is . . . *people* . . . people are

like bars . . . or like a drink. There's acceptance there. If you don't like a drink you accept it and move on, but if you like the drink you keep going back to it. Marius was someone I always wanted to go back to. One of the good ones . . . and he is damn sure worth the return." I paused again.

"I am an only child . . . so Marius was like a brother to me . . . there was this one time when I was living in New York in a ten-by-ten-foot room with a loft bed and I had been working at a heavy metal bar in the neighborhood where the patrons could only pay in cash but were allowed to do all this illegal shit in the bathroom. The owners, two brothers, kept a long massive chain on top of the bar at all times as a notice to *cut out* the stupidity. One night I witnessed one of the brothers swing that chain like a helicopter blade . . ." I unsnapped my shirt and started furiously swinging it around. " . . . and slash some drunk jackass in the face while the older brother laughed the entire time." Someone threw me an orange Malanx jersey. "I felt safe at this bar . . . " Most faces in the crowd were blank.

" . . . and I know a lot of you feel the same way . . . so, if I had a glass in this ridiculous place I would raise it to you . . . to Marius." I raised my hand in the air anyway as if it were a cocktail. "Here's to you, Marius. You're the best. The best gentleman I know."

Some people sitting down in the crowd actually raised imaginary glasses as well. Leonard seemed to raise his glass higher than anybody.

"And finally, we want to play a song," I said, slipping the Phalanx's jersey over my head and giving Mike his cue. "It's a song that Marius liked a lot."

> . . . *ah-oh, smokestack lightin'*
> *shinin' just like gold.*

The music rang out and the crowd moved out to the lawn of the parlor to bleed into the group outside, and all I could see was a sea — hundreds of intertwined orange jerseys dancing and gyrating.

> *... whoa-oh, tell me, baby*
> *where did ya' stay last night?*

> *... whoa-oh, stop your train*
> *let her go for a ride*

> *why don't ya' hear me cryin'?*

Victoria was slow-twirled by Leonard, and Hillary alternated half humps on Mike and Richard. Officer Carr had Jackie up close, and that orange wave slow-danced and blues-swayed in enchanted undulation; there were many hugs and embraces, cigarettes and slight ponderous pauses. I smoked one cigarette after another as joyous people came up to me crying and laughing.

> *... whoo hoo*

Leonard put his arm around me, still holding hands with Marius's mom. "You did damn good in there, boy. Couldn't have said it better. Only wish we had actual drinks to raise it to."

"Soon enough," I said.

Chad Carr came over to where I was standing, asked me if I had a minute, which of course I did. We walked a few paces to a tree on the side of the building away from the crowd.

"I asked around, had the autopsy looked at again. Seems there's no explicit foul play. Just his blood contained lethal level for heroin overdose, but barely ... I'm sorry ... I wish Marius had never gotten into injecting that stuff."

"It's okay." I grabbed him on the shoulder and looked him in the eye. "There are some things that people don't need to know . . . it was an *accident*. Best now to let it go."

"You sure? I can keep investigating this, ask around."

"No, you've done enough. There's been enough *asking around*. Best to just breathe again. Thank you." He gave me a warm handshake. "Say hello to your wife for me."

"Will do. Take care of yourself, Bjorn."

Merle walked over to me, I ground out my cigarette and I pulled her in close as the music played. We slowly danced and she said into my ear, "Why don't you stay around a while."

Feeling her beautiful comfort, it was tempting. "Nah. I still have some work to do on my own. There's this place I need to get to . . . but I'll be back. I haven't given up on this place."

She reached up and kissed me, and I leaned down and kissed her back.

"Where's Vance?"

"We're taking a break," she said, and I didn't ask any further. Only pulled her to me and started to resume the slow dance adjacent that orange sea, her soft face on my shoulder.

We danced like that into that humid evening, and there wasn't much else to say. What can you say? A friend dies and you just move along. You mourn for him, even at times envy him because you are left to deal with the bullshit — all of the toils and imperfections and absurdity, all the little things that can just about drive you batshit.

And well after midnight after Merle and everyone else had left, Leonard was quiet for a change as he and I, still both drunk after the alcohol arrived, walked up to the Triumph parked outside the parlor.

Finally, he asked me, "Now what are you going to do?"

"Not sure yet. Think I might take this thing past Denver. Always wanted to live in Colorado."

"Just a brokeass drifter."

"Shit, you would hardly leave Houston if the place was getting the hydrogen bomb."

"Shit," Leonard said, "it comes to that I might as well just jerk off into the radioactive cosmos."

"You were always good for a one-liner."

"You're welcome."

"But you'll always be here, and that's actually worth something. It's good to know."

Leonard put a hand in my shirt pocket and took out one of my cigarettes. "Aw, shit. A compliment for the old man?" *Calm-plo-mint*. "I done heard it all now." He looked at me. "It's like I always told Patsy when we was going through our shit. You go to the bar and you do what you do . . . but you always come home."

"Poetic," I said.

Leonard sipped a Coke bottle filled with bourbon. "That there was Confucious."

"Confusing," I said.

As I got on the cycle, I told him: "Well, old man. This is it. Guess I will be seeing you later."

He ashed his cigarette onto the street. "Just keep your nose clean, Bjorn."

"Same to you. Try to drink more V8." He inhaled, blew smoke into the polluted tongue of sky. I grinned and gave him a handshake. "So long, you homophobic racist."

"Until the next shitstorm," he said.

"Well, shit, I love you too." The glorious son-of-a-bitch, sores and all — just an unlikely angelic beartoad with a dangling cigarette and a long scroll of pros and cons. He grinned that joker's face I had learned to accept. "I guess we're just from a family of losers," I said.

"Nah we ain't. But losers somethin' though, boy. Losers have more endurance. The goddamn winners die in car wrecks, get killed by camel humpers — then get their names in neon lights and parties like the one tonight." I smiled back at him.

So they do, old man.

So they do.

#21

about a year later

In the Rockies now, some people call them that — I call them the bardo in high altitude — I sit here sober and clear-eyed and healthier, thinking about that weekend plus overtime.

He was right. They all were. As is everyone. Everyone was right. Today, tomorrow. *Then*.

I meant what I said that night: I do love my father. And I appreciate my family and look forward to getting to know all of them better one day — to returning home after this wandering around.

After this respite.

Pretty soon, I think I might call that girl named Merle, invite her up here. Maybe I could show her some snow without shit.

The truth is I have great compassion for my city. From afar and now. Good people there, we know that.

Though I do miss my friend, this is also true.

Learn from my mistakes. Your mistakes. Willie Nelson is singing *Shotgun Willie* in my background, my foreground, my everything—but I don't have a gun around in these Rockies.

Only this damn lighter in the bardo.

But of course I still have a long way to go for graciousness yet . . .

. . . but until then patrons of the excess bound . . .

. . . I'll repeat what I screamed to that enkindled radiance of orange Houstonians that Sunday night after the lunacy and violence, after some kind angel had finally shown up with a few thousand cans of Lone Star, a brick of hash, and more than enough bourbon to kick that Texan evening of Howlin' Wolf along—right before I got fucked up just that one last time.

"Dance, you motherfuckers! Dance!"

Get out there and gag your heart. Get it all out. Gag out the negative. Make it all new. For the grace of it and you and everybody.

Puke today.

Rest tomorrow.

"You'll be perfect."

. . . whoo hooo

Dr. Hank Anderson
1980-2015

Right after my good friend Hank died in a freak accident on a summer sunny day in between Durango and Denver, I wrote the first draft of this story in a kind of cathartic fever dream. For subsequent drafts, during holiday breaks and smoke breaks in between my regular jobs — between the summer of 2015 in Lafayette, Indiana, and summer of 2020 in Corvallis, Oregon (with a couple of years in Seattle thrown in there for drizzly measure) — I spent by my best estimation about 1,000 hours on this thing (and probably needed a thousand more). **THANKS** to my buddy Grant Whipple, Artist-at-Large, for designing the cover for this book, and **MANY THANKS** to these wonderful people who helped me write this book, one way or another, during those thousand hours: Sharon Moore, James Moore, Jim Moore, Penny Brown and my many fabulous Texas cousins, Tootsie Moore, Brian Commender, Nancy Commender, Mark Ross, Kiko Serna, Tony Duran, Adam Lefton, Mark Mengel, Lee Causey, Jesse Donaldson, Scott Waugh, Ashlee Waugh, Abe Anderson, D'Lorah Long, David Murphy, Eli Green, Mike Ferguson, Ryan Brown, Stephen Monteiro, Stacey Swann, Owen Egerton, Adam Corson, Erin Corson, Skand Bhatt, John Larison, Wayne Glausser, Keith Scribner, Justin St. Germain, David Turkel, and Rob Drummond. Love you all.

SPECIAL THANKS to Erica Fischer and Ezhno Martin. Both all-star saints with pretty mouths.

Walter Moore has a BA in English from DePauw University, an MFA in Creative Writing from Texas State University in San Marcos, and a Ph.D. in American Studies from Purdue University. A published poet and journalist (and occasional screenwriter and actor), he's taught English at the college level for seventeen years (and he's had a bunch of other crap jobs along the way & in between). He now lives in Eugene, Oregon, and teaches in the School of Writing, Literature, and Film at Oregon State University. Though he's lived in over twenty towns/cities around the world, he's a fifth-generation Texan and considers Houston, Texas, as his hometown. His book of poems, ***My Lungs Are a Dive Bar*** was released in 2019. He loves to dance, especially with his lady-friend Erica and friend-beast Lloyd.

CPSIA information can be obtained
at www.ICGtesting.com
Printed in the USA
LVHW041732220321
682103LV00011B/2455